Gordy was still on the ground when his two attackers tried to leave with his banner. He held one by the leg, but the other took the pole from the banner and swung it hard. It caught Gordy right across the back of his head and sent him spinning into oblivion.

By the time the ambulance arrived, he was lying unconscious in the road in a pool of blood.

Other titles in the City Hospital series

X-RAY

KEITH MILES

HarperCollinsPublishers

First published in Great Britain 1996
by HarperCollins*Publishers* Ltd
77-85 Fulham Palace Road, Hammersmith,
London W6 8JB

Copyright © Keith Miles 1996

The author asserts the moral right to be identified
as the author of this work.

ISBN 0 00 675221 7

Set in Stempel Garamond
Printed and bound in Great Britain by
Caledonian International Book Manufacturing Ltd.,
Glasgow, G64

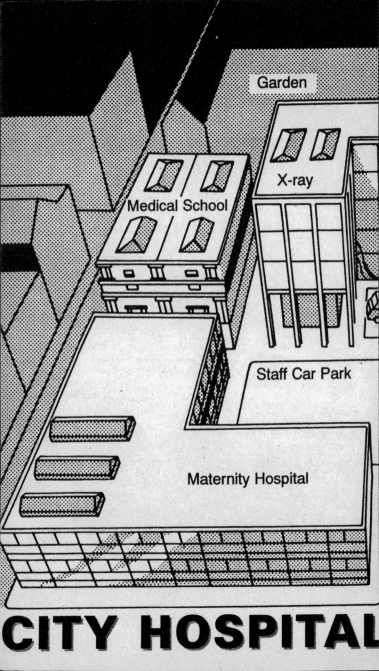

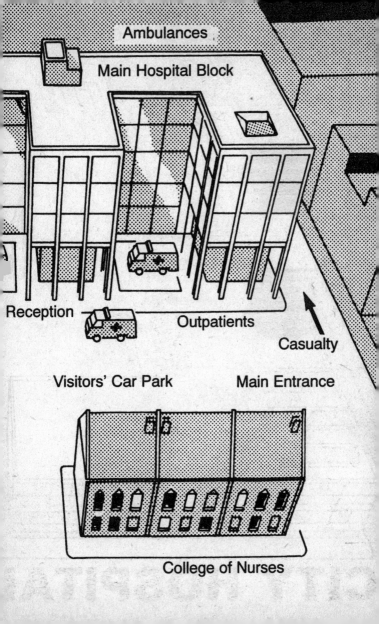

Ambulances

Main Hospital Block

Reception

Outpatients

Casualty

Visitors' Car Park

Main Entrance

College of Nurses

It was to be a peaceful demonstration. When Gordy Robbins agreed to join it, he hadn't expected it would end in a riot. He'd never been on a march before and the only reason he went on this one was to please Kirsty Longdon. Right now, most of his spare time was taken up with thinking how he could please her.

'Help me to unroll this, Gordy,' she said. 'It's a banner. We'll carry it between us on the demo.'

'OK. What's it say?' asked Gordy.

He soon found out. When the banner was unfurled, its message was written in huge red letters.

ANIMAL WELFARE PROTEST MARCH

'They want us at the front,' said Kirsty, 'where everyone will see us.'

'Can't we just lose ourselves in the crowd?' asked Gordy, mildly alarmed.

'But Gordy, it's great to be asked to lead the protest,' said Kirsty. 'And you said you were keen to help.'

'I am, Kirst, I am. I'd do anything to help you, and the Animal Welfare cause. You can call on me any time.'

'You're wonderful, Gordy!' Kirsty's eyes were shining.

When she looked at Gordy like that, he went weak at the knees! Kirsty was a knockout. She was tall and slim and sophisticated, and had the kind of inner beauty which shone out whenever she smiled. Kirsty was Gilbert Buchanan's secretary – and he was the leading surgeon at City Hospital. She had dozens of medical students after her, but Gordy was the one she'd chosen to go out with.

'You're different from the others,' she said now. 'You really care about serious issues.'

'You're right, Kirst!' he lied. 'Animal Welfare is very important to me. Equal Pay for Pigs and Cattle, I say!' he joked.

'None of my other boyfriends could stand Dodo, either,' she explained. 'But since you love animals, you'll get on great with her.'

'Dodo?' asked Gordy, warily.

'Yes,' she said. 'My dog.'

Kirsty crossed the road to a lamp post and untied a large Dalmatian. The dog wagged her tail and licked Kirsty's hand enthusiastically. She tied the dog lead to her belt and Dodo trotted behind her, obediently.

'This is Gordy,' said Kirsty to her dog.

Gordy tried to sound friendly. 'Hi, Dodo!'

She growled at him, threateningly. This dog

could become a problem.

'OK! Get ready, everyone!' boomed the organiser through his loud-hailer. 'Get in groups behind Kirsty and her friend.'

Gordy suddenly felt self-conscious, as nearly two hundred people came towards him. They were a mixed bunch: there were young people, a cluster of middle-aged women and several pensioners – there was even a man in a wheelchair. Many of them had brought their pets along, too. They were a peaceful group of demonstrators and only a handful of policemen had been assigned to escort them along the High Street.

Gordy looked over his shoulder at another banner being hoisted by a couple of students in jeans.

BAN LIVE ANIMAL EXPORTS

And further back he saw a slogan he, too, felt strongly about.

STOP EXPERIMENTS ON ANIMALS

Gordy was grateful that the laboratories at City Hospital didn't use live animals for their experiments – it was something he opposed fiercely.

'Right!' said the man with the loud-hailer. 'Make sure you wave your banners and make plenty of noise. Give out those leaflets to anyone who'll take them. We've got to get our message across. OK – let's go!'

A big cheer went up as the marchers set off, four abreast, in an orderly column. Gordy and Kirsty led the way with their banner held high. Dodo loped along behind them, barking noisily. The rest of the demonstrators began to chant:

'Ban Live Exports! Spare Animals Pain!'

Kirsty started to chant, too, but Gordy kept quiet. He felt out of place; all he wanted to do was to get the march over with so that he could slope off somewhere and be alone with the lovely Kirsty. His real interest was Gordy's Welfare!

Everything was going smoothly until they turned into the High Street. It was a busy afternoon and small crowds of people stopped to stare at the marchers. Some shouted encouragingly but a few jeered. One or two even joined in the march. But what surprised Gordy was the sight of a television crew, filming the march for the local news. Since he was in such a prominent position in front of the march, Gordy was bound to be picked out. He hated the idea of being seen by any of his mates at medical school. They'd really tease him.

'Hold the banner higher, Gordy!' shouted Kirsty.

'Sorry,' he said, straightening his pole immediately.

'Isn't this fantastic?'

'Yes, Kirst. It's great – I'm really glad I'm here,'

he called back.

'We're striking a blow for the Animal Kingdom!' said Kirsty.

Dodo growled at him again and Gordy felt like striking a blow at the dog, but that certainly wouldn't be in the spirit of the occasion. He soldiered on, trying to hold his arm up to obscure his face from the television camera. They were halfway down the High Street now, and as they reached the end, they would swing right into the town square to listen to some speeches from the organisers about animal welfare.

They were passing the end of a lane when it happened. Twenty or more youths suddenly charged out into the High Street and started to attack the demonstrators and tear down their banners. Gordy and Kirsty were their first targets. Two stocky youths in jeans and sweatshirts grabbed at their poles.

'Let's get that down, mates!' shouted one.

'Stop them, Gordy!' screamed Kirsty.

'Hey! What d'you think you're doing?' said Gordy, clinging on to his pole as one guy tugged frantically at it. 'Let go!'

'You're asking for trouble, mate,' he warned.

Kirsty's pole was wrenched out of her grasp but Gordy wasn't going to give up without a fight; other marchers took the same view. As the youths tried to grab their banners and seize their leaflets, the demonstrators fought back. It was chaos. The police jumped in to help but a fresh surge of attack came from another side street, causing a riot! The noise was deafening.

Gordy was determined not to let go of his pole and he was fighting hard. His hefty attacker was getting increasingly menacing.

'Let go or I'll smash ya face in!' he yelled.

'It's our banner!' Gordy shouted.

'Don't let go, Gordy!' cried Kirsty.

'Right!' breathed the youth. 'You asked for it!'

Instead of tugging at the pole, he began to thump Gordy with both fists and Gordy dropped the banner to defend himself. The march was out of control as confusion erupted in pockets all over the place. Men were roaring, some of the women were screaming and the children were crying as the police yelled commands that went unheard and unnoticed.

When the first brick went through a shop window, the riot intensified. People were thrown to the ground, banners were torn up or set on fire, leaflets were scattered all over the street and any bystanders were badly pushed and shoved in the throng of people. More bricks were thrown and there were even people clambering through shop windows and snatching anything they could lay their hands on. The march was being used as an excuse for theft and violence. Although the police had called for reinforcements, they arrived too late to stop the damage.

While Gordy was tussling with his attacker, Kirsty snatched the banner protectively. A big man, with long hair tied in a pony tail, tore it out of her hands. As he did so, Dodo bit him hard and he kicked out. Kirsty tried to get her banner back but she was thrown to the ground.

'Gordy!' she cried. 'Help me!'

Pushing one of them away, Gordy flung himself at the other, knocking him over. Nobody was going to hurt Kirsty while he was around! She struggled to her feet, encouraging Gordy, but now he was up against two of them. They both began punching and kicking him.

The wail of more police sirens finally dispersed the attackers, and they began to break away, running back down the lane. But Gordy was still on the ground when his two attackers tried to leave with his banner. He held one by the leg, but the other took the pole from the banner and swung it hard. It caught Gordy right across the back of his head and sent him spinning into oblivion.

By the time the ambulance arrived, he was lying unconscious in the road in a pool of blood.

CHAPTER TWO

Mark Andrews loved being a student nurse but what he enjoyed most was the practical experience on the wards. Staff shortages were always a problem at City Hospital, and the students were often drafted in to fill a gap somewhere. This time, Mark was especially pleased – he'd been told he was to be assigned to the Maternity Hospital again – even though he would only be given the most boring tasks to do.

Mark was wheeling a trolley along the corridor when he heard a voice calling behind him.

'Excuse me!' she called.

Mark turned round with a smile. 'Can I help you?' he asked.

'I hope so. Can you tell me where the Ante-Natal Clinic is?'

'Yes, it's on the ground floor. These are the labour wards and delivery rooms up here.'

'Oh,' said the young woman, smiling. 'I'm not ready for them just yet!'

The girl was short and round, with rosy cheeks. She had brown hair which rippled down to her shoulders – and she looked about nineteen. Mark noticed the vivid colours she was wearing –

her purple sweater was covered with the signs of the zodiac in gold thread and her tie-dyed jeans were tucked into bright red boots. She wore an orange headband, a necklace of large beads and dangling silver earrings. Her fingers were covered with rings and Mark saw that she was heavily pregnant.

'Is this your first visit, then?' he asked, surprised.

'Yes,' she said. 'We've only just moved into the area – there weren't many maternity hospitals near Stonehenge. We've been taking part in some festivals – we're travellers – New Age travellers.'

'Oh I see. Have you got a place to live here, now?'

She smiled again. 'Well, not exactly. We've got a converted double decker bus – that's home to all six of us. My name's Jasmine, by the way. And yours?'

'I'm Mark, Mark Andrews, I'm a student nurse here, helping out in the Maternity Hospital.'

'Hi, nice to meet you, Mark. Is it OK, this hospital?' she asked.

'Yes, it's great – it's a teaching hospital so the facilities are excellent. Especially in Maternity.'

Mark smiled at her, reassuringly.

'I'm glad to hear it. I didn't fancy giving birth in the middle of Salisbury Plain. I mean, I love the outdoor life but not when it comes to having babies. It's the usual thing,' she sighed. 'We don't actually live here, we're not on the electoral roll, and so on. Honestly, Mark, people can be so officious! We're parked on a disused caravan site, only a couple of miles away, so I'm entitled to come to this hospital, aren't I?'

'Of course you are,' said Mark. 'That's what the National Health Service is all about.'

Just then, two nurses appeared and gave them a friendly smile as they walked past. Jasmine sensed an atmosphere of calm efficiency that reassured her.

'They seem nice enough,' she said.

'Yes, they are,' said Mark. 'And they don't only care about the mothers, they take a real interest in the fathers, as well. In fact, they encourage the dads to be present at the birth, if possible.'

'Not where I'm concerned, I'm afraid. I'm not sure I know who the father is!' She winked at Mark. 'It could be Baz or it could be Raphael.' She shrugged, laughing. 'It doesn't make much difference, really.'

'It will to the baby, Jasmine.'

'But Baz and Raphael will both look after it, anyway. So the baby will have *two* fathers.' She giggled infectiously. 'Hey, maybe they'd *both* like to be there when the baby's born. Do you think the hospital would allow that?'

Mark felt rather shocked. He'd never really met anyone quite like Jasmine before.

⎯⋏⎯

'What exactly happened, Gordy?' Karlene Smith was asking.

'I wish I knew!' he said, ruefully. 'It was supposed to be a peaceful demonstration – famous last words!'

'How are you feeling now?' asked Suzie Hembrow.

'Well, I'm still a bit dazed.' he admitted.

'What did the doctor say, Gordy?'

'He's keeping me in overnight – as a precaution.'

Gordy was propped up in bed in City Hospital. He had several stitches in the gash in the back of his head, and some severe bruising on his face. Bandages covered most of his forehead, and there were abrasions on his arms and body from rolling on the ground in the High Street during the fight.

Karlene and Suzie, both in uniform, had come to see him as soon as they'd heard the news. Gordy's memories of the march were hazy, but he did remember some things.

'I couldn't let them push Kirsty around,' he said, angrily. 'Those two thugs – they looked like soccer hooligans. The kind that enjoy aggro for its own sake. Breaking up a peaceful demo was their idea of fun!'

'Did they hurt Kirsty?' asked Karlene.

'Well, one of them wrenched the banner from her hands and shoved her on the ground. Kirsty yelled for me to help and I jumped on the guy.' He rubbed his aching head. 'That's about all I can remember. Then someone must have hit me.'

'You were very brave, Gordy,' said Karlene, admiringly.

'Yes,' added Suzie, 'it sounds to me as if you were a real hero!'

'A fallen hero, Suze.'

'Well, I'm sure Kirsty must be proud of you.'

'But where is she now?' said Gordy, concerned. 'Kirst ought to be here: I'd never forgive myself if she'd been injured as well.'

'She wasn't,' reassured Karlene. 'Damian Holt would have told me. He was on duty in Casualty when you were carried in. Damian rang the Physio Department to tell me you'd been caught up in a riot. If Kirsty had been admitted then, he'd have seen her for sure.'

'I agree,' said Suzie. 'Casualty treated several people from the march with minor injuries. Kirsty definitely wasn't with them.'

But Gordy was still anxious. 'Then where's she got to?'

'Just relax, Gordy. She'll be along soon. Don't worry.'

'Yes,' said Karlene, adjusting his pillows. 'You need plenty of rest. Just lie back, Gordy, and take it easy.'

'Yes,' agreed Suzie. 'You've earned a nice long sleep.' She looked puzzled. 'But what I can't understand is how you came to be on the march in the first place.'

'Kirsty invited me,' said Gordy.

'But I thought you had a lecture this afternoon?'

'I skipped it, Suze. I told the professor that I had an urgent dental appointment.' He felt his jaw tenderly. 'I nearly did, too. That thug tried to knock all my teeth out. And I had no anaesthetic!'

'I didn't know you were a keen supporter of Animal Welfare,' said Suzie.

'Not as keen as he is on Kirsty,' teased Karlene. 'If she'd asked him to march in support of Home Rule for Hypnotists or Bus Passes for Bank Clerks, he'd have gone, wouldn't you, Gordy? He'd take up any cause to be next to Kirsty.'

'That's not fair, Kar,' said Gordy. 'I've always liked animals. I had a golden hamster when I was a kid, until I swopped him for ten comics and an ice lolly. But I looked after him while he was mine,' he said, defensively. 'I cleaned his cage out every day.'

'A true Animal Welfare activist, like Kirsty, would say that he shouldn't have been in a cage at all. They believe all animals should have freedom. Not be stuck behind bars in a zoo, or be made to do silly tricks in a circus.'

'I'd go along with that, Kar.'

'Since when?'

'Since I first thought seriously about it.'

'Since you met Kirsty Longdon, you mean.'

'Don't tease him,' said Suzie. 'He's not up to it. Gordy needs to be looked after. We ought to be waiting on him hand and foot.'

'Thanks, Suze,' he said, pathetically.

'Sure there's nothing you need, Gordy?'

'Yes,' he said. 'A rope ladder so that I can climb out of here! Hospitals are fine when you're working in them or just visiting. But this place is giving me the creeps now I'm trapped in it.'

'It's only for one night, come on!'

'But they might keep me in for a week! A month even!'

'Not with the shortage of beds we've got,' observed Karlene, drily. 'The physio will have you up at dawn and the doctor will boot you out by lunchtime.'

'Then we can look after you,' said Suzie.

'That'd be nice, Suze, but I'll go back to medical school as soon as I'm discharged. I daren't miss two afternoon lectures in a row, the professor would kill me! I'll just have to pray that he doesn't watch television this evening – Kirst and I are on the news.'

'How do you know?' asked Karlene.

'There was a television crew there, filming the march. They're bound to have some scenes of the riots. My professor thinks I went to the dentist, so what do I tell him if he sees me fighting in the middle of the High Street?'

Karlene thought hard. 'Say that you've got a twin brother.'

'Oh yes – and how do I explain this bandage round my head?'

'The dentist got a bit angry with you?' she suggested, helpfully.

'My professor will get a bit angry with me if he realizes I missed a lecture to carry a banner in a protest march for Animal Welfare.'

'Cross that bridge when you come to it,' advised Suzie. 'The main thing is, that you get a good night's sleep after your ordeal. You were knocked unconscious, Gordy. That's bound to make you feel weird.'

'True, Suze. My head's still pounding.'

'We'll let you get some rest.'

'Thanks for coming,' said Gordy.

'We'll be back later,' promised Karlene.

'Yes,' added Suzie, 'and Mark and Bella will want to come as well. They're the nurses. You'll get star treatment from them, Gordy.'

'The only person I want to nurse me is Kirst. I wonder where she is?'

'Still fighting in the High Street, maybe?'

'Not her. She's a pacifist, Suze.'

'Kirsty is?'

'Yes, she doesn't believe in violence.'

'Not even in self-defence?'

'She wouldn't harm a fly,' said Gordy, confidently. 'One thing's for sure, Kirsty would never get involved in a punch-up like that.'

———/\/———

Kirsty had never been inside a police cell before. It was scary. It was small and bare and cold. A barred window was set high in the wall, and the steel door had a rectangular panel in it. Every so often, someone lowered it and peered in at her before clanging it shut again. Kirsty felt even more distressed; it was as if she was like one of the animals she'd been on the march for, locked up in a cage for human inspection.

The fear and isolation would have been easier to bear if she'd had Dodo with her. But the police had taken the dog away somewhere, and Kirsty could hear her barking plaintively in the distance. Where had they put her? But anxiety about Dodo was quickly overtaken by her concern for Gordy. He'd been so brave! To protect her, he'd taken on two strong thugs and he'd been hit over the head for his efforts. Kirsty felt very responsible for his injuries, and if Gordy suffered any lasting damage, she knew she would be to blame.

She was only in the cell there for half-an-hour, but it felt like a lifetime, when suddenly the hatch opened and a pair of eyes examined her. As it was slammed shut again, a bolt was drawn back and the door swung open. Kirsty jumped to her feet.

'Where's Dodo?' she asked the police sergeant, fiercely.

'Who, Miss?'

'Dodo's my dog.'

'She's fine,' said the sergeant. 'We've popped her in one of the kennels until we get you sorted out.'

'But I didn't *do* anything!' she pleaded.

'That's not what WPC Ridley says.'

'We were having a peaceful, legal demonstration until we were attacked.'

'And then you lot hit back,' he said.

'We defended ourselves, that's all.'

'Oh yes,' said the sergeant. 'Very violently, by all accounts. The charges against you are quite serious, young lady. Causing a fight in a public place, damage to property and assault on a woman police officer. You're in serious trouble.'

Kirsty stood there and shivered.

'Gordy!' she whispered. 'Where are you?'

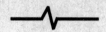

It was raining hard when Bella Denton left City Hospital and she was glad that she had an umbrella with her. A swirling wind made life even more hazardous. She walked along the pavement and dodged the puddles as best she could. Traffic was thick along the main road – moving slowly because of the poor visibility – when the driver of a Mondeo became frustrated and tried to overtake the line of cars ahead of him. His wheels sent up a spray that soaked pedestrians.

As he went past Bella, he hit a pool of water in the road and created a small tidal wave. Bella was drenched.

'Hey!' she protested. 'Look what you're doing, can't you!'

It was then that the accident happened. As the traffic lights turned red, the driver jammed his foot hard down on the brake and his car skidded along the wet surface and into a spin. A young boy on a mountain bike was directly in its path. He tried to get out of the way but he was too slow. When the car hit him, he was knocked flying; his mountain bike crushed under one of the car's wheels.

'Oh, no!' gasped Bella.

She was furious with the man driving so dangerously, but her main thought just then was for the victim. The traffic had halted in all directions, so she ran out into the middle of the road where the boy lay, motionless. A small crowd had gathered around him and he was beginning to moan. Bella knelt down beside him.

'Are you all right?' she asked.

'My leg!' he groaned. 'It's my leg!'

'Somebody call an ambulance!' she shouted.

A man in a delivery van used his mobile phone to dial 999 and two other drivers had jumped out of their cars and were having a go at the man in the Mondeo. Soon a fierce argument developed and horns began to beep in the waiting queues of traffic. The crowd around the boy got larger and more vocal.

Bella held her umbrella over his head to keep off the rain. He was no more than ten or eleven, and his teeth were gritted against the severe pain: his whole body was shivering. His right leg was twisted at an unnatural angle and blood began to seep from a bad gash on his temple. Bella put her umbrella to one side and tore off her coat to cover him. The noise around her seemed almost deafening. Just then, she heard a decisive voice which cut straight through the chaos and commotion.

'Move aside, please! I'm a doctor!'

The crowd parted and a tall, fair-haired young man pushed his way through, a black doctor's bag in his hand. He assessed the situation quickly and set about reassuring the young boy.

'You're going to be fine, son, don't worry,' he said, as he examined his injuries. 'You just lie there until we can get you away in an ambulance.' He turned round. 'Please! Move back! Give the boy some air.'

As the crowd edged away, the young man took off his own coat and rolled it up to make a pillow, slipping it gently under the boy's head, taking care not to touch the injuries on his temple. He opened his bag and ripped the plastic wrapping off a pad which he used to stop the bleeding. He took Bella's wrist, and guided her hand on to the pad.

'Hold it there, firmly,' he said.

'Yes, doctor.'

'Now, my lad. Let's have a look at you.'

The young boy was clearly in agony but the doctor had obviously managed to calm him. Bella felt reassured, too. He clearly knew what he was doing and was handling the boy with great care as he tried to determine the nature and extent of his injuries. With the hospital so close, it only took a couple of minutes for the ambulance to appear, its siren wailing down the road. A police car arrived, too, from the opposite direction, and soon two policemen had jumped out and were moving the traffic along so that the ambulance could get through to the boy.

'You're a lucky lad,' decided the doctor, at last.

'Is he OK?' asked Bella.

'Yes. He's going to have a nice long break from school, but when he goes back, he'll be as good as new.'

The boy smiled bravely and the doctor patted his arm. The ambulance nosed its way through the crowd and soon the paramedics were inspecting the boy and lifting him gingerly on to a stretcher, strapping him on and covering him with a blanket. The doctor told the paramedics his diagnosis, then talked softly to the boy as he was lifted into the ambulance. Only when the vehicle had pulled away did Bella realize how soaked through he was.

'Put this back on,' she said, holding out his coat.

'Oh, thanks, yes.'

'You were great – taking control like that.'

'It was just lucky I was passing,' he said.

Instinctively, they moved together to the shelter of a shop doorway. The police had got the traffic moving again and were studying the site of the accident. They had moved the shattered bicycle out of the way and were talking to the driver of the Mondeo, who sat, white-faced and guilty, giving his statement.

Bella and the doctor were putting their coats back on.

'Thanks for your help,' he said, smiling. 'I don't always have a nurse at my side like that.'

'I was on my way home from the hospital,' she told him.

'Then the boy was doubly lucky. He gets knocked off his bike and, hey presto, there's a doctor *and* a nurse standing by.'

'It was awful – he didn't stand a chance,' said Bella.

'Did you see the accident?' asked the young doctor.

'Yes,' she said, pointing at the car driver. 'It was *his* fault. He could have killed that boy!'

She turned to take a proper look at the young man for the first time. He had a long, thin, intelligent face and warm brown eyes. He was wearing a dark suit under his coat and Bella liked his sense of quiet authority. The Irish lilt in his voice made him even more attractive.

'My name's Doctor Mullen,' he said. 'Carl Mullen.'

'I'm Bella Denton,' she said. 'Student nurse

and soaked to the skin!'

'We need somewhere to dry out,' he said, looking around. 'Is there a café nearby?'

'Yes, on the next corner, doctor,' said Bella, beginning to shiver from the after-effects of the accident.

'Can I buy you something to warm you up?'

'Please!' she said. 'A nice strong cup of tea!'

'Just what the doctor ordered. I'll go on ahead and get them while you give your statement to the police. All the other witnesses seem to have gone now.'

'Well, I'm here and I'm ready to tell them *exactly* what I saw!' she said, defiantly.

'See you in the café then, Bella.'

'OK, thanks—'

'Carl,' he said. 'No need to be formal. Please, call me Carl.'

'Right,' she said, happily. 'I will, Carl.'

———⋀———

Suzie was about to leave the X-ray Department when one of her tutors walked in. Geraldine Hobson was a big, handsome woman in her thirties with a warm, maternal manner.

'You're late this evening, Suzie,' she said.

'I took an hour off this afternoon, to visit a friend of mine in Chesford Ward,' explained Suzie.

'So I thought I'd make it up at the end of the day.'

'I wish everyone had your dedication,' said Geraldine, drily.

She opened the door of the storage unit and searched through a rack of X-rays. Each one had a sticker to show the name and number of the patient, the type of X-ray, the date when it was taken and the name of the relevant consultant. A set of initials showed which radiographer had been responsible for the X-rays. Precise details were essential for the efficient running of the department. Geraldine didn't seem to be able to find the ones she wanted. 'Do you remember a Mr McVitie?' she asked.

'Yes,' said Suzie. 'He came in this morning for a chest X-ray. He went in to see Joan Cross. Why?'

'I can't seem to find his X-rays,' she said, puzzled. 'They should be here, in alphabetical order.'

'They usually are – let me have a look. Maybe they got put in the wrong place. I'll check everything we've had in today, Geraldine.'

And so the two of them went through the dozens of X-rays which had been taken that day – but without success. Mr McVitie's X-rays were nowhere to be found.

'They *ought* to be here,' said Geraldine, irritably. 'Who was in charge of putting them in the storage unit today?'

'Hayley was – Hayley Jansen. But she left an hour ago. She'll be in tomorrow, you could speak to her then.'

'But the consultant wants to see those X-rays now. His secretary has just rung down for them. What am I supposed to tell him? That the set's gone missing?'

'They must be here *somewhere*,' said Suzie, running her hand along the rack. 'Maybe they've got mixed up with yesterday's batch. I'll go through the whole lot, OK?'

'Thanks, Suzie. Let's do it together.'

They both searched thoroughly, but it was no use. Suzie shrugged. Geraldine was obviously very annoyed.

'Where *can* they be?' she said.

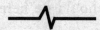

From his hospital bed, Gordy had heard the sound of the ambulance bringing the injured boy into Casualty, but he hadn't noticed it. All his attention was concentrated on his visitor – Kirsty had finally turned up to see him.

'I'll never forget what you did, Gordy,' she was saying.

'Nobody touches you while I'm around,' he said, proudly.

'That vicious thug hit you with one of the poles from the banner! He might have split your head in two!'

'I feel as if he did, Kirst.'

'You poor thing!' said Kirsty, sympathetically.

She put a gentle hand on his brow and he seemed to revive miraculously. Kirsty was full of sympathy and he wanted to make the most of it.

'I'm sorry I couldn't get here before,' she said.

'I thought you'd abandoned me,' said Gordy, trying to look pathetic.

'I'd never do that, Gordy. No, I was locked up in a police cell.'

'What!' he exclaimed.

'I don't know why: I didn't do anything. They said I was involved in the riot.'

'We all were, Kirst. But not from choice. It was those hooligans who started it.'

'I suppose I did get a bit carried away,' she admitted. 'When I saw what they were doing to you, I began to hit out, wildly. I wanted to save our banner. Unfortunately, a policewoman got in the way.'

'You mean – you hit her?'

'Well, so she *claims*. Anyway, they arrested me and Dodo.'

'What have they charged the dog with?' asked Gordy, joking.

'They put her in kennels while they locked me up in the cell. It was horrible, Gordy! I felt as if I was in a kennel myself.' She shuddered.

'It must've been awful for you, Kirsty.'

'It was. They released me, pending charges,' she said. 'They want to look at the video evidence of the riot first.'

'So do I,' said Gordy, with feeling.

'Oh? Why?'

'To see who smashed me with that pole.'

'It was that big, nasty-looking guy with glasses and a woolly hat,' said Kirsty.

'Would you recognize him again, do you think?'

'Yes, I think so.'

'Karlene's going to record the news for me – there's bound to be some pictures of the riot. I want to see if I can spot exactly who that guy was.'

'And then?'

'I'll go after him, Kirst.'

'I should leave that to the police, Gordy.'

'No way! It's me they hit. Besides,' he said, 'coppers make mistakes. We get assaulted by a gang of maniacs and who do they lock up - you! An innocent victim. I can't forget what happened. I want revenge. Those guys won't be allowed to get away with this, I'll find them!'

'But it's too dangerous, Gordy!'

'Don't worry, Kirsty, I can look after myself,' said Gordy, showing off.

'I know you can!' said Kirsty, affectionately. 'You were fantastic on that march. You're a star, Gordy!'

Kirsty leaned over and kissed him on the cheek. Gordy looked delighted. Revenge could wait until he'd recovered. There were more important things just at the moment.

'You can count on me, Kirst,' he affirmed. 'Even if it means another bang on the head.'

'Oh no!' she protested. 'I don't want you to get hurt again.' She held his hand, stroking it gently. 'What I'd really like to do, is take you back to my flat and look after you properly. I could be your nurse. I could really show how grateful I am then.'

'Get the Ward Sister straight away, so I can discharge myself and come home with you now!'

'You can't do that, Gordy.'

'But you just said it's what you want,' he protested.

'Well... it is I suppose.'

'So what's stopping us, then?'

'It's Dodo. I'd love to have you back to my flat but she gets very possessive. She wouldn't allow you anywhere near my front door. Let alone the bed. Sorry, Gordy. It just wouldn't work.'

Gordy was amazed. 'Are you telling me I take second place to your Dalmation?' he wailed.

'I'm afraid so.' Kirsty looked resigned.

Gordy shut his eyes in utter disbelief.

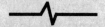

CHAPTER FOUR

The coffee bar was crowded but he managed to find a table in the corner. When Bella arrived, she dropped her umbrella in the stand and hung up her coat. Adjusting her uniform, she crossed over to Carl with an apologetic smile

'I look like a drowned rat!' she said, sitting down.

'You look fine, Bella. Drink your tea.'

'I really need this!'

'Have you given your statement to the police?' asked Carl.

'Yes – that Mondeo driver should be put away.'

'It's lucky the accident wasn't fatal.'

'That poor boy – I couldn't bear to look at his leg,' said Bella, shuddering.

'You'll get used to that kind of thing in time.'

Carl Mullen sipped his coffee and studied Bella with interest. Even with her dark hair plastered to the sides of her head by the rain, Bella looked very attractive. He was intrigued by her perfect features, pure white teeth and olive complexion.

'Where are you from, Bella?'

'I'm studying at City Hospital.'

'No, which country, I meant.'

'I was born and brought up here,' she said. 'My father's English but my mother's Malaysian. I have a lot of relatives out in the Far East.'

'No need to tell you where I'm from, is there?' Bella smiled at him.

'It's Dublin, to be exact,' said Carl. 'I've just qualified and my mother bought me this doctor's bag as a graduation present. She wanted me to be a GP in Dublin, though.'

'So what are you doing here?'

'Looking for a job. I decided it was time to spread my wings – Ireland's too small for me. I decided I want to work over here.'

'As a GP?'

'I don't know yet,' he said, vaguely. 'I want to consider all my options first. I've had two interviews so far, both with practices in the city. But I've also applied for a job at your hospital. I was on my way there when the boy was knocked off his bike.'

'You're going to work at City Hospital?' said Bella, looking pleased.

'Well, only if I'm offered a post.' He grinned at her. 'I'm still waiting to hear. In the meantime, I was going to take a look at the place, see how the land lies, sort of thing.'

'I could show you around,' Bella volunteered. 'I could even sneak you into the College of

Nurses.'

'That sounds fun!'

They smiled at each other again. The crisis seemed to have drawn them together. The more Bella looked at Doctor Carl Mullen, the more she liked him. The idea of having him at City Hospital was an irresistible one.

'When will you hear?' she asked.

'Any day now.'

'You'd *love* it there – I know you would.'

'I certainly like the bit of it I've already seen!' he said, enthusiastically.

'Oh? What's that?'

'You, Bella.' He grinned again.

She laughed. Bella had a weakness for young doctors. She wasn't going to let Carl walk out of her life yet when she'd only just met him. He certainly had the Irish charm.

'When do you want the grand tour?' she asked.

'Any time. I'll fit in with you, Bella.'

'It'll have to be in my lunch hour. But you could phone me at home or at the hospital. I'll give you both numbers, you're bound to find me at one of them.'

'I'll do just that,' said Carl, looking delighted.

She gave him the two numbers and he jotted them down on the back of an envelope and slipped them into his pocket.

'You'll have to give me your number, as well,' she said.

'I don't have it with me just now, Bella. I'm staying at a little hotel near the city centre. But I'm on the move a lot,' he said, evasively. 'It'll be much easier if ring you.'

'OK. Do you promise?'

'Sure I do, Bella! Put it this way,' he said, leaning across the table. 'Nothing will stop me from ringing you, and I'll do my best to persuade you to have a proper drink with me – either in a pub or a wine bar, OK?'

'Great, Carl! I wouldn't need much persuading!'

'Now, tell me everything there is to know about the hospital,' said Carl. 'If I do get an interview, I want to be well-prepared.' He put a hand on her arm. 'Go on, Bella. Give me the lowdown.'

Karlene had also worked late at the hospital that evening. She'd been helping to take a group of elderly patients through some exercises in the swimming pool. Her tutor, Catherine White, looked on approvingly as Karlene and another student, Zack Hilliard, encouraged the swimmers from the side. When the session was over,

Catherine intervened, thanked her two students, and helped them with the task of getting the patients out of the water.

When the last patient had gone to the changing rooms, Karlene was left alone with Zack.

'This swimming pool's a marvellous thing to have,' she said.

'Yes,' he agreed. 'I hadn't realised how valuable it would be for physiotherapy. That group of patients has improved so much you'd hardly recognize them, and it's only been a couple of weeks.'

'That's because we're such hard task masters, Zack.'

'Firm and friendly – that's our motto.'

'You're beginning to sound like Catherine White.' Karlene laughed.

'But she's the best physio in the hospital, isn't she?'

'Yes, I know. She does seem to have that magic touch.'

Zack was a tall, angular young man with thick brown hair. Like Karlene, he was keen to learn and always volunteered for extra duties. Most of the time, he was quite a live wire but he'd been very subdued during this session. Karlene thought he must be over-tired.

'I know what I'm going to do now,' she said.

'Put on my bathing costume and dive straight into that lovely warm water. How about you, Zack?'

'Not today, thanks.'

'But you usually like a dip.'

'But not this evening,' he said, stubbornly.

'Are you taking Hayley out tonight?' asked Karlene.

'No,' he said. 'I've got too much work to do.'

'Well, a swim might help you relax.'

'I'm just not in the mood, Karlene. The pool's all yours. You can practice your diving. See you tomorrow.'

'OK. Bye, Zack!'

She waved as he walked away, but she felt puzzled. Zack was a really good swimmer and he usually seized every opportunity to swim in the hospital pool. Why hadn't he wanted to this time? Karlene was mystified.

———⋀———

Suzie was making breakfast in the kitchen when she heard a van pull up outside the house. She glanced through the window and saw the name of the hospital written across the side. Suzie realized it was one of the vehicles they used to carry outpatients to and from the hospital. But what was it doing in their street?

The front door opened and then she knew the answer.

'Gordy!'

'Hi, Suze!'

'What are you doing here?'

'The hospital needed the bed so they kicked me out.'

'So soon?'

'It was my idea,' he explained. 'I didn't want to spend another night in that place. There's nothing seriously wrong with me, after all. I only had a bang on the head. So I persuaded the Ward Sister to release me.' He grinned at her.

'You sound as if you're out on parole.' Suzie gave him a welcoming kiss and ushered him through to the kitchen. His eyes lit up at the sight of the bacon and eggs in the frying pan.

'Is there enough for me, Suze?'

'You can have it *all*, Gordy. You get VIP treatment at the moment.'

'That's worth coming home for,' he said, flopping down on to a chair. 'Where is everybody?'

'It's early so they're still asleep. I'll give them a shout in a minute. Let me take a proper look at you.'

Suzie bent over Gordy and examined his injuries. He was still wearing a bandage round his head and the bruises on his face were beginning to turn yellow. He sighed apologetically.

'Sorry, Suze. I look like Frankenstein's monster!'

'No you don't, Gordy,' she told him. 'Well, no more than usual, anyway!' They laughed. 'You were lucky to have no permanent damage. Those bruises will fade in a few days.'

'I need them to fade by this afternoon!' he said. 'I can't walk into a lecture like this. My mates'll tease me like crazy and the professor will ask why my visit to the dentist made me look like a boxer.'

'Don't go to the lecture then,' suggested Suzie.

'I have to, Suze.'

'OK,' she said, 'but what you need is cosmetics!'

Gordy winced. '*Make-up?* That's for girls!'

'Guys can wear it as well.'

He shuddered. 'You'll have me in a dress and a pair of high heels next! I don't want people whistling at me!'

'Make-up would hide those bruises, Gordy. You can get special lotions that camouflage marks like that. They use a whole range of them at the hospital mortuary!'

'Thanks a lot!' said Gordy, jumping up. 'I'm not dead yet, Suzie. And I'm not going to wear any corpses' make-up!'

'Calm down,' she said, easing him back into his seat. 'I'm just trying to help. When can you take that bandage off?'

'Right now. It's only protecting the wound on the back of my head. They said to leave it on, but I want it off now. I'll comb my hair over the stitches.'

'Let me give you a hand.'

Suzie undid the bandage, unwinding it carefully. There were no cuts on Gordy's forehead and he already looked much better. She put the bandage on one side and examined him closely.

'Some foundation would take the colour out of those bruises,' she suggested, 'and a spot of powder on top would work wonders.'

'What else? A pair of earrings and a handbag?'

'Don't be silly, Gordy. If you want to conceal those facial marks, that's what you should do – nobody would ever notice,' she promised.

'*I* would, Suze!'

'What about a tan then? Just a light suntan – to cover your whole face.'

'Are you crazy?' he yelled. 'I can't go sunbathing in weather like this!'

'You don't have to, Gordy. Fake tan comes out of a bottle from the chemist. It would give your face an all-over, even colour.'

'So would a couple of coats of paint!'

'Be serious.' She shook her head at him.

'I am. No make-up! I'd be much too embarrassed.'

'No you wouldn't. Think about it, Gordy.'

———⋀———

As soon as they reached the Maternity Hospital, they set to work. Mark and Bella stripped all the beds and put the dirty sheets into a large, wicker laundry basket. They wheeled it down the corridor towards the service lift. Bella was still talking dreamily about Carl Mullen.

'He's fantastic, Mark!'

'That's what you always say, Bella.'

'But this time it's different.'

'And you say that, too.'

'Carl's special. He's a doctor.'

'So's Damian Holt,' he reminded her. 'There was a time when *he* was out of this world, as well.'

'Don't be so cynical, Mark.'

'But you exaggerate, Bella.'

'Well I'm not this time. Really, he could be the right one for me!'

Because he liked Bella, Mark didn't rise to any more of her comments. When she was on the verge of a new romance, there was no holding Bella back. It was always the same. She couldn't talk about anything else. They pushed the basket into the lift.

'Just think!' she said. 'He might come and work here!'

'What? Changing the beds?'

'No! As a consultant.'

'I thought he'd only just qualified,' said Mark, as the lift descended. 'It takes ages to become a consultant.'

'Carl will make it. You wait! He's brilliant.'

'He certainly seems to have rescued that kid on the bike. Have you been to check on him yet?'

'Of course!' said Bella. 'He's got a broken leg and three fractured ribs. I really hope they prosecute that driver!'

The lift stopped and the doors parted. As they pushed their basket along the corridor, Mark saw a familiar figure at the reception desk. She was wearing the same colourful clothing as before.

'Hi, Jasmine!' called Mark.

'Oh, hi!' she said, turning to smile at him.

Mark introduced Bella, and the girls shook hands.

'What are you doing back here so soon?' he asked.

'Searching for my earring.' Her hand went up to her ear. 'It must have come off when I was doing those exercises in the Ante-Natal Clinic. They were quite strenuous!'

'At your stage of pregnancy?' said Bella, surprised.

'The exercises weren't energetic but I *did* them strenuously,' explained Jasmine, giggling. 'I'm hyperactive. At least, that's what Baz says. And Raphael, too.'

'Who are Baz and Raphael?' asked Bella, amused at the look of this zany girl.

'Oh, they're friends of mine, and one of them's the father of my baby. We won't know who until it arrives,' she said, winking.

'How will you be able to tell for sure?' asked Mark.

'Just wait till you meet Baz and Raphael. Then you'll see what I mean.' She thought a moment. 'Listen, why don't you come to the party! We're having one tomorrow night, Mark. It'll be great. Bring Bella along, too. The more the merrier!'

Her infectious laughter echoed along the hospital corridor.

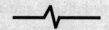

───∿─── CHAPTER FIVE ───∿───

Suzie arrived early at the X-ray Department and changed into her uniform. The first person she saw was Hayley Jansen, another student radiographer.

'Good morning, Hayley.'

'Hi, Suzie.'

'Back on the treadmill again!' Hayley nodded, wearily. 'How did you get on last night? You went to a disco with Zack, didn't you?'

'I was going to,' said Hayley. 'But he didn't want to go in the end. He said he just wasn't up to it.'

'Is he ill or something?'

'I don't know – he looked all right to me. He said he had to work so I just watched telly all night. I was bored out of my tiny mind.'

Hayley was a striking and attractive Jamaican. She was tall and graceful and she'd been a successful athlete at school. Suzie had always envied Hayley her glowing fitness. She was a close friend of Suzie's house-mate, Karlene, and the two of them had a lot of laughs whenever they went out together. But there was no sign of her sense of fun now.

'I was really fed up,' admitted Hayley. 'I'd

brought a new dress to change into so we could go on to the disco from here, and what happens? Zack rings me from Physio and says it's all off.'

'He could have given you more notice,' agreed Suzie.

'That's what I told him. Just be thankful you haven't got a boyfriend, Suzie. I just hate being messed around. Zack Hilliard had better watch his step!' She smiled suddenly. 'Sorry, Suzie, I didn't mean to let off steam at you.'

'That's OK,' said Suzie, easily. 'Talking of letting off steam, even Geraldine did that yesterday. I've never seen her get so angry. It was about some missing X-rays,' she explained. 'Apparently, they belonged to a Mr McVitie. He came in yesterday morning for a chest X-ray. I remember him; I took him in to Joan Cross and then she handled things from there.'

'Yes,' agreed Hayley. 'When Joan processed the X-rays, she gave them to me to put in the storage unit.'

'And did you do that?' asked Suzie.

'Of course I did! I put them in alphabetical order, under M for McVitie.'

'Well, they weren't there, Hayley.'

'But they *must* have been.'

'I searched, and Geraldine searched, and we couldn't find them. She was hopping mad. One of the consultants was shouting for them and they'd vanished! Geraldine's afraid we'll have to get the patient back in again, to re-do them all.'

'I'm sure there's no need for that,' said Hayley. 'I'll find them for you right now. Come on!'

Hayley led Suzie to the storage unit and unlocked the door. She looked at the rack of X-rays from the previous day and ran her finger along them. Then she lifted out an envelope of X-rays and held it up.

'Here they are, Suzie,' she said.

'Are you sure those are Mr McVitie's?'

'Yeah. Henry Alexander McVitie.'

Suzie was baffled. 'Where *were* they?' she asked.

'Exactly where I put them yesterday,' said Hayley. 'I don't want to be rude, but you and Geraldine need to have your eyes tested. The X-rays were here all the time.'

———⋀———

A full day at the Maternity Hospital meant Bella had little time to think about Doctor Carl Mullen. She was kept very busy – but she didn't mind. It was all good experience for a student nurse and she met a lot of interesting people. She'd liked Jasmine on sight. The young traveller had a style and manner that Bella admired. As for Baz and

Raphael, Bella was dying to meet them. But she sensed Jasmine was playing a bit of a joke on them. Life in their converted double-decker obviously wasn't dull!

At the end of the day, when she left the building, her thoughts went back to Carl. Would he really call, or had he just taken her phone numbers out of politeness? She had no way of contacting him. Bella was cross with herself for not getting the name of his hotel. But there couldn't be all that many small hotels near the city centre. All she had to do was to call each one and she was bound to find him, eventually.

But there was no need. As she crossed the hospital car park, she saw him standing outside the main block. Bella couldn't believe it at first; Carl was glancing through a magazine as he waited. It was dry today so he didn't need a coat and he was wearing a different suit, but he had his doctor's bag beside him. Bella started to run towards him.

'Carl! Carl!'

'Oh hi, Bella!' he said, looking up and smiling. 'It's really nice to see you!'

Before she knew it, she'd landed in his arms, and he kissed her cheek.

'I was hoping to catch you,' he said, laughing. 'Remember that job here at the hospital?'

'You've heard from them?'

'I've been short-listed,' said Carl, looking pleased.

'That's wonderful!' said Bella, grabbing his hands. 'When's the interview?'

'The end of the week.'

'I knew you'd get the job!'

'Hold on a minute, Bella,' he said, laughing at her over-excitement. 'There are three other candidates and they've probably got equally good qualifications.'

'Not from where I'm standing,' she said, looking at him appraisingly.

He smiled. 'Thanks, Bella. Are you on your way home? Because I could walk back with you,' he suggested.

'That would be great, Carl.'

He rolled up his magazine and slipped it into his bag before they set off towards the main gate. Bella felt so happy. Here she was, walking along with this dishy young doctor – it was more than she'd ever expected.

'What was the magazine you were looking at?' she asked.

'The *Lancet*.'

'That's too advanced for me.'

'I like to keep up with the latest developments in medicine,' he said. 'There was an article on heart transplants; they've made so much progress in that area. One day I'd love to be involved in that kind of work.'

You already are, thought Bella. My heart has just been transplanted. She cleared her throat. 'So you want to be a surgeon?' she asked.

'Eventually.'

'You'll have to work at a hospital, then. And ours is as good as any.'

'Well, you can show me around then, Bella. How about lunchtime, the day after tomorrow? Bella Denton, tour guide. I bet you know everything about the hospital there there is to know!'

'I do actually, Carl. Especially in the Maternity Hospital.'

'Can you get me in there to have a look around?'

'Easily. You can see whatever you want.'

'I'll start with you,' he said. Bella laughed.

'Actually, there was another reason I came along today. I wanted to see the boy who had the accident. So I popped my head in to check on him.'

'How is he today?' asked Bella.

'He's rather uncomfortable,' said Carl, 'but he's on the mend. He was more worried about the damage to his mountain bike than about his broken leg. I cheered him up by telling him he'd probably get a brand new bike from the driver's insurance company.' He looked at Bella. 'By the way, he's so grateful to you, Bella. You were the first person to help him.'

'I did my best,' said Bella.

'A textbook response. Quick, informed and effective.'

'I'm just pleased he's going to be all right.'

They were silent as they approached the crossroads where the accident had taken place. The traffic was moving smoothly now but Bella could pick out the exact spot where the boy had landed after being struck by the car. There were deep scratches on the road, made by the handlebars of his bike as it dragged along the surface. She looked away.

They were well past the junction before Carl spoke.

'How was your day, Bella?'

'I was rushed off my feet as usual.'

'The real thing will be far worse,' said Carl. 'When you're a qualified nurse,' he said. 'How do you fancy working long nights?'

She pulled a face. 'Everybody has to take their turn. That's what Sister Killeen always says. She's our tutor – one of the old school.'

'And Irish, by the sound of it.'

'Just like you, Carl. You ought to meet her.'

'No, thanks. The only nurse I'm interested in is you.'

Bella was so happy she reached out and put her hand through his arm. She felt so comfortable with him as they strolled along, it was as if they'd known each other for ages. He seemed very relaxed in her company, too.

'Have you always wanted to be a doctor?' she asked.

'Yes – I feel I was born to it, Bella.'

'Do you come from a medical family then?'

'Yes,' he said. 'My father was a GP and two of my uncles were consultants in Dublin. I even have a sister-in-law who's a hospital manager. My father died a few years ago and my mother wants me to carry on where he left off.'

'But you don't want to stay in Ireland?'

'No, Bella. I wanted to work here first. It was the only way I could get to meet you!' he joked. 'Do you believe in destiny?' he asked.

'I didn't. But I do now,' Bella confessed. 'We turn down the next road. You must come to the house and meet the others.'

'I'll have to leave you here, I'm afraid.'

'But they're dying to see you, Carl.'

'Another time maybe.'

'They're my friends,' she said. 'Gordy's going to be a doctor one day. Then there's Mark, another student nurse, and Karlene, she's a trainee physio. And Suzie, of course, who's the boss really, she's training to be a radiographer.'

'A full hospital staff under one roof!' said Carl.

They stopped at the corner and Bella was disappointed not to be able to take him to meet the others – but she knew that he must be busy.

'Till the day after tomorrow, then,' she said.

'I'll give you a ring to confirm it,' said Carl. 'What is the name of your hotel?'

'The Hazelmere.' He kissed her goodbye. 'But I've moved out of there now.'

Before she could ask why, he'd gone, and was striding down the road away from her. Bella watched until he'd disappeared round the bend. She was desperately sorry for the boy who'd been hit by the car, but the nasty accident had had the nicest possible result for her. Bella had met Carl Mullen and her whole life had suddenly changed!

———⋏———

Gordy carried the banner high, with his arm obscuring his face. Kirsty was holding the other pole, with Dodo the Dalmation at her heels. The camera focused on the slogan – ANIMAL WELFARE PROTEST MARCH. Then the mob arrived. A gang of youths charged across the road in a bunch and flung themselves at the demonstrators, trying to tear down their banners and disrupt the march.

Gordy pressed the remote control button to freeze the frame.

'There, Kirst!' he said, pointing. 'See him?'

'That's the one who hit you with the pole!' she cried.

'Are you really sure?'

'I'm *certain*, Gordy.'

He let the video continue. It was very brief; the camera panned up and down the column of marchers to show the extent of the riot. Whenever Gordy came back into view, he was wrestling with one of the youths who'd attacked them. They saw Kirsty pushed to the ground and Gordy going to help her. They even saw the moment when the pole was smashed across the back of Gordy's skull.

'Oooh!' he said, turning away. 'I felt that!'

'They should charge him with Grievous Bodily Harm.'

'They have to catch him first, Kirsty.'

They were alone in the living room together. Gordy had invited Kirsty back to the house that evening to watch the recording Karlene had made of the local news the previous evening. She'd insisted on bringing Dodo, but Gordy didn't mind. The dog had curled up on the floor and gone to sleep. Now, snuggled up on the sofa with Kirsty, he put his arm around her. Reliving the attack brought them closer together than ever.

'At least I know who hit me now!' said Gordy.

'What a coward!'

'I'll get him, Kirst. One way or the other, I'm determined to find him.'

'That video is all the evidence you need.'

'There's no sign of you hitting a policewoman, Kirst.'

'But these are only edited highlights,' she said.

'I know,' Gordy sighed, 'but it was still possible to identify me very clearly. My professor did just that. He was really angry because I'd skipped his lecture.'

'Animal Welfare is more important than lectures!' said Kirsty, vehemently.

'Try telling him that!'

'I hope you didn't get into trouble because of me, Gordy. Whenever I look at your injured face, I feel so guilty. Do those bruises hurt much now?'

'Not when I'm close to you, Kirst. Maybe you should kiss them better.' Gordy pulled her towards him and kissed her lips. They were soon locked in a warm embrace – but it didn't last long! Before Gordy could really enjoy the moment, Dodo came back to life, barking noisily. They drew apart instantly.

'Poor Dodo!' cooed Kirsty, stroking her. 'She hates to be left out, don't you?'

Gordy groaned. 'Well I'm certainly not kissing *her*!' he said.

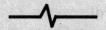

CHAPTER SIX

Karlene kept a close eye on Zack that morning. He seemed unusually subdued. He and Karlene were helping to take patients through their exercise routines in the hospital gymnasium. Karlene was as enthusiastic as ever, praising each small advance in mobility that her patients made and encouraging them. But Zack lacked energy – his mind clearly not on his job.

As he headed for the canteen at lunchtime, Karlene walked beside him and tried to cheer him up.

'Lisa Tomkins is doing really well today,' she said. 'You remember, that little girl whose arm was crushed. Didn't you see how much she'd come on – you've worked wonders with her, Zack. Her arm's working almost normally now.'

'Yes,' said Zack. 'Lisa has done well. But it was the surgeon who put her arm together again, not me.'

'But you're the one who helped rebuild her confidence. Lisa was very upset when she first came to us.'

'That's true. It's a pity, she's a nice kid.'

'A few more weeks and her arm will be like

new. She won't let you down, after all you've done for her, Zack.'

Karlene saw him smile for the first time that day. It was a positive sign. Zack was very committed to physiotherapy and really got involved with his patients. It was very rewarding that they placed such trust in him.

In the canteen, they saw Hayley at an empty table. She waved at them as they drifted across to her. Zack gave her a peck on the cheek.

'I saved you a couple of seats,' said Hayley.

'Thanks,' said Karlene. 'We'll just get some food.'

'I'll get it,' offered Zack. 'You stay here and chat to Hayley. What do you want, Karlene?'

'Tuna salad, please. And a large orange juice.'

'They're on their way. Pay me when I get back,' said Zack, moving towards the serving hatch.

While he joined the queue at the counter, Karlene sat down opposite her friend. Hayley looked wistfully at Zack.

'How's he been today?' she asked.

'A bit quiet, really.'

'That's just not like him.'

'I know,' said Karlene. 'He's almost as noisy as you as a rule.'

'Nobody's *that* noisy,' said Hayley with a grin. 'I can make more noise than anyone I know when

I really get going! It's one of the things that Zack used to like about me – he called it my effervescent personality.'

'He still does like that side of you, Hayley.'

'I'm not so sure, Karlene.'

'He cares about you – you know that.'

'I don't think so, not any more.'

'Of course he does. He's just going through a phase, that's all.'

'Yeah,' sighed Hayley. 'A Get-Rid-Of-Hayley phase.'

'Come on – don't be silly!'

'But look what happened yesterday!'

'He wasn't in the mood to go to a disco, that's all.'

'Zack's *always* in the mood. That's why he's such a great guy. He's the only boyfriend I've ever had who can out-dance me. When I'm with him, life's really exciting, Karlene.'

'He feels the same about you, you know he does.'

Hayley looked across at Zack, who was starting to load plates on to the plastic tray. She sighed and lowered her voice as she confided in her friend.

'It's been going on for over a *week*, Karlene. He's just not interested anymore,' said Hayley, sadly. 'He hasn't touched me, Karlene. I'm sure that's the reason he didn't want to go to the disco. We usually finish up at my flat and Zack stays the night. It's great! At least, it was until now.'

'He's crazy about you.'

'Then he's got a funny way of showing it. Listen, can I ask you a big favour, Karlene?'

'Sure, go ahead.'

'Talk to him,' said Hayley. 'You work with him all day so you can choose the right moment. Find out if he really has gone off me, will you? I've got this feeling Zack's going to dump me because he's got some other girl.'

'You're crazy!'

'Just talk to him, Karlene, please. See what you can find out. Only be tactful, don't tell him I put you up to it, he'd hate that!'

'Leave it to me, Hayley.'

'Thanks! You're a real friend, Karlene.'

—/\—

It was a long walk from the bus stop and they ended up walking through a confusing maze of streets. Mark and Bella were on their way to Jasmine's party and Mark was very curious to meet her friends. But Bella's mind was fixed firmly on someone else.

'He could be a second Gilbert Buchanan,' she said.

'Who are you talking about?'

'Carl, of course.'

'Give him a chance, he hasn't even got a job yet!'

'He'll go straight to the top, I know he will.'

'Bella, it takes *years* to work your way up,' argued Mark. 'Gilbert Buchanan's in his sixties. And he's unique. He really is the top surgeon in his field.'

'Carl will be like that, I bet you anything. There's something about him.'

'You said the same thing about Damian Holt, remember?'

'Forget Damian, will you?' she said, irritably. 'He's not in the same league as Carl.'

'As a doctor or as a boyfriend?' teased Mark.

Bella stuck her tongue out at him. She'd clearly fallen for this young Irish doctor and it wasn't kind to tease her.

'I just hope he realizes how lucky he is, Bella. You're very special. Even Sister Killeen admits that. Just make sure Carl appreciates you! Now, when do we get to meet this Mister Wonderful?'

'I don't want to rush things, Mark. We've only just met. We need to give things time to develop.'

'Time to develop!' Mark laughed. 'I like that. You've already got him taking over Gilbert Buchanan's job, by the end of the week you'll have Carl running the World Health Organisation. That's not exactly giving him time to develop!'

'I was talking about our *relationship*, Mark!'

As they turned a corner, they saw the double-decker bus in the fading light. It was parked on a site that had once had permanent caravans, but it was something of a rubbish dump now. There were huge piles of litter everywhere and an abandoned car lay, desolate, in the far corner. They could even see an old stove and a kitchen sink – it was hardly the most salubrious place to live.

'What a place to bring up a child!' said Mark.

'They won't stay here for ever, I'm sure. They're travellers, after all. People like Jasmine always keep on the move – hence their name. They're rolling stones.'

They could hear the music clearly now – the bus was positively throbbing to New Age sound. Whoever had decorated the outside of the bus had real talent; the signs of the zodiac were painted in all colours, set against a red background and linked with New Age motifs. It was an amazing sight. Mark and Bella stood gazing at it for a moment before they went into the party.

'There you are!' shouted Jasmine. 'Welcome!'

'Hi!' said Bella. 'What an incredible place!'

'It's great!' added Mark. 'Here, we brought

you a bottle, Jasmine.'

'Fantastic, thanks!'

Jasmine gave them both a kiss and took the bottle. They had no idea so many people could be squeezed into such a small area. It was heaving. Some people were drinking, some were dancing and some were standing talking. A lot of the girls wore colourful clothes with necklaces, bracelets and huge earrings.

'Leave your coats upstairs!' said Jasmine above the noise. 'I'll get you both a drink. Hurry up!'

'Right,' said Mark. 'Lead the way, Bella.'

'This is great, isn't it?' she said.

Three double mattresses took up most of the space upstairs, with only a thin curtain between each. Mark and Bella left their coats on the pile.

'How many people actually live here, Mark?'

'Six,' he said. 'Not much privacy, is there?'

Bella grinned. 'I don't think Jasmine cares too much about privacy.'

Downstairs, Jasmine handed them both a glass of wine, then dragged two people out of the crowd to introduce them.

'This is Baz and this is Raphael,' shouted Jasmine above the din, her arms round both of them. 'Mark and Bella, from the hospital.'

Both the guys were very different. Baz was short and stocky with a bald head and a fair beard.

He had three small rings through his right nostril. Raphael was tall, slim and dark with long black hair. An arm grabbed Baz and yanked him back to dance.

'That's Ellie,' explained Jasmine. 'Baz is with her now. And I'm with Raphael.' Raphael grinned amiably. 'It's worked out really well so far.'

'Dance, Jasmine?' Raphael asked.

'Sure!' said Jasmine, holding his hand.

'Is that OK?' Mark looked alarmed. 'Shouldn't you be taking it easy by now?'

'That's hard for me, Mark!'

'A gentle dance won't matter,' said Bella, smiling.

'There's nothing gentle about the way *I* dance,' said Jasmine with a giggle. 'If the baby decides to come early, I've got two nurses standing by. It's one of the reasons I invited you!'

The music got louder as the two of them edged their way to the centre of the party. Jasmine and Raphael were soon dancing enthusiastically. Mark looked at Bella and then they both burst out laughing. Jasmine was irrepressible!

$$\diagdown\!\diagup$$

Another morning was beginning in the X-ray Department. When Suzie had changed into her uniform, she found a memo addressed to her. It was from her tutor Geraldine, asking her to take a set of X-rays over to the Orthopaedic Clinic. Suzie noted the patient's name and went straight to the storage unit. She was soon flicking her way along the rack to find the relevant X-rays. But they weren't there. She checked the name again, then had a second and more intensive search. She still failed to find what she was looking for.

Puzzled and annoyed, she went to the reception area. Hayley had just arrived, carrying a large plastic bag and looking weary.

'Hi, Suzie,' she said in a lifeless voice. 'I wish you weren't so bright and breezy this early in the morning.'

'I don't feel bright and breezy,' said Suzie. 'I've started the day with a bit of a problem.'

'What's that?'

'Some more X-rays are missing.'

'They can't be.'

'They are, Hayley. Geraldine wants me to find the set belonging to a Mrs Vincent, and they're not there.'

'Mrs Vincent? Wasn't she in yesterday?'

'That's right.'

'Then the X-rays should be exactly where I put them.'

'But they're not. I've just been looking for them.'

'They *must* be, Suzie. That storage unit is kept locked. X-rays can't just walk away. I'm sure I can find them. Wait here.'

'No, I want to come with you,' insisted Suzie. But before she could move, she saw Geraldine bearing down on her. Hayley went to the storage unit on her own and the tutor beckoned Suzie over to her.

'Did you take those X-rays to Orthopeadic?'

'Not yet, Geraldine.'

'Well do hurry up. The consultant's got an appointment with that patient first thing. He needs those X-rays now.'

'That might be difficult. You see, I couldn't find them.'

'Aren't they in the storage unit?' Suzie shook her head, looking worried. 'Not another set going astray! This is unbelievable!'

'I've looked everywhere, Geraldine.'

'We have to find them, Suzie! It's essential.'

'Hayley swears she put them in there yesterday.'

'Well, where is she now?'

'Right here,' said Hayley, walking back into reception with a set of X-rays. 'This is what you want I think – Carolyn Mary Vincent – taken yesterday. They were on the rack, right where they should be.'

'Thank goodness!' said Geraldine. 'How on earth could you have missed them, Suzie?'

'I really don't know.' Suzie looked stunned.

'Well race them over to Orthopaedic, at once!'

'Yes, right away, Geraldine.'

'Want the name of a good optician?' Hayley whispered to Suzie as she passed.

'That might not be a bad idea,' she said, baffled. 'I must be going blind.'

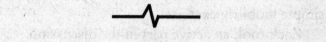

CHAPTER SEVEN

The day began with a seminar led by Catherine White. She was talking about the value of physiotherapy in post-operative patients. Karlene and the others were told that even patients who'd undergone heart by-pass operations, should be got out of their beds at the earliest opportunity for simple mobility exercises.

Zack took an active part in the discussion.

'What happened before physios came along?' he asked.

'There were extended periods of convalescence,' said Catherine. 'Even a routine operation for appendicitis might put you in hospital for two or three weeks. Heart surgery would involve months of convalescence. And that could lead to another problem.'

'Hospital became their home?' suggested Karlene.

'That's right. Patients became institutionalized. They had to employ medical social workers to prepare them for their return to the outside world.' Catherine smiled proudly. 'That's all in the past, thanks to physios – patient turnover has sped up considerably.'

It developed into a lively debate with everyone taking part. Karlene had to wait until their mid-morning break before she had a moment alone with Zack. She bought him some coffee from the machine and crossed to their small staff room.

'We learn something new every day,' she said. 'You certainly had plenty to say, Zack.'

'It was an interesting topic.'

'Only to a physio, I bet.'

'What do you mean?'

'If I was a patient who'd had major surgery, the last thing I'd want is two keeny-beanies like us, hauling me out of bed to stagger around the room. Bring back convalescence!'

'Would you want to spend that long in hospital?'

'Not really, no. I'd be bored in a week!'

'Then physiotherapy *is* the answer.'

They sipped their coffee, chatting about their schedule for the rest of the day. Karlene gradually managed to work the conversation around to Hayley.

'How does she keep so fit I wonder?' said Karlene. 'She looks like an advert for health food. She glows with energy. Does she work out in the gym?'

'Sometimes. We play squash quite often, too. And she goes jogging – she's a really good athlete.'

'I feel like a slouch beside her.'

'But you're as fit as anyone, Karlene.'

'Don't look too closely,' she said with a grin. She changed the subject slightly. 'It's lasted quite a while now, hasn't it?'

'What has?' asked Zack.

'You and Hayley – I can't seem to keep a boyfriend for more than a few weeks. What's her secret?'

'She's a great girl,' he said, almost under his breath. Zack was staring straight ahead of him. Karlene watched him for a while and saw real signs of strain around his eyes. Whatever he was thinking, it was troubling him a great deal. She saw his jaw tighten.

'What's the problem, Zack?' she asked. 'Something's worrying you, I can see.'

'No it isn't.'

'I know you too well, Zack.'

'There's nothing wrong with me,' he snapped, defensively.

'Then why have you been acting so strangely lately?'

'What are you on about, Karlene?'

'I care about you,' she said, softly. 'I'm interested, that's all.'

'It's a pity you don't care enough to leave me alone.'

'Zack!'

'*She* put you up to this, didn't she?'

'Who?'

'Hayley,' he said, getting to his feet. 'She asked you to spy on me. That's what this is all about, isn't it?'

'Of course not!'

'Just leave me alone, will you?'

Glaring at her, Zack turned and walked quickly out of the room. Karlene swallowed hard. She'd handled it really badly. Hayley wasn't going to be pleased when she heard about it.

———⋀———

'What's down there?' asked Carl.

'ENT – Ear, Nose and Throat.'

'Let's skip that,' he said.

'I can get you in there if you like,' said Bella. 'I know one of the receptionists.'

'You seem to know everyone in the entire hospital.'

'I suppose I do. I like to get around.'

'I think I've seen all I need to see. You're a great guide, Bella. You've shown me everything I asked you to at City Hospital.'

'So what's the verdict?'

'I'd recommend you to any visitors.'

Bella laughed. 'About the place itself,' she said.

'Do you still want to work here or I have put you off completely?'

'Oh, I'm more determined than ever to get that job.'

'That's great, Carl!'

Bella had spent almost an hour showing him round the complex. Carl was fascinated. He plied her with questions about the running of the hospital – his interest never seemed to flag. When they glanced into wards and treatment rooms, he was able to identify medical equipment that Bella didn't even recognize herself. She'd never met anyone who seemed to know so much about so many things.

'There's such a distinctive atmosphere here,' he said.

'It's the smell of disinfectant,' said Bella, making a face.

'It's more than that, Bella. Hospitals have their own aroma – when I inhale it, I feel completely at home.'

Bella grinned at him. The last hour had been one of the most enjoyable she'd had since coming to the hospital, and all she'd done was walk around it. Being with Carl was a treat in itself. She'd never been short of boyfriends, but he made all the others seem very shallow.

'You're really dedicated, Carl,' she said,

'wanting to come to an inner city hospital like this. It's in a rough area with every social problem you could name. Yet you really want to work here.'

'This is where it all happens, Bella.'

'Some of Gordy's friends don't think like that.'

'Is Gordy the one at the medical school?'

'Yes,' she said, 'and he's as committed to the NHS as you are. But some of his friends can only talk about how much they'll make in private medicine. They want to have rooms in Harley Street and make a fortune.'

'That's not for me. I became a doctor to help people, not to make money. Isn't that why you became a nurse?'

'Yes, that's right. It's a vocation for me.'

'That's why we get on so well – we're kindred spirits.'

'I feel that, too.'

She looked at him intensely. Suddenly, her eye was caught by the sight of the clock, on the wall behind his head, and she gulped.

'Help! Is that really the time? I'll have to go.'

'What about your lunch?'

'I'll have to forget that. I'm back on duty at two.'

'You can't go without lunch, Bella.'

'I'll have to.'

'Then let me make it up to you,' he said. 'I'll

take you out for dinner tonight. How does that sound?'

'Great!'

'Seven-thirty then, outside the town hall?'

'I'll be there!'

'Terrific. Now, get over to Maternity as fast as your legs can carry you.'

Bella started to run down the corridor. 'And thanks again!' she called.

'See you tonight!'

Bella was so happy. She'd have gone without food for a week to have dinner with Carl. Their friendship was getting better all the time.

'Sit still, Gordy!' she said. 'Or I'll smudge it.'

'Sorry, Kirst.'

'I've almost finished.'

'Are you sure Gilbert Buchanan won't come in?'

'It's his day off.'

'But someone else might walk through the door.'

'It's locked, Gordy. Now, don't move.'

Gordy had been horrified when Suzie had suggested make-up to cover his bruises. But when Kirsty came up with the same idea, he suddenly saw its advantages – the main one being that she would act as his beautician!

It was the end of her working day and he'd come to her office. Kirsty was waiting with a tray of make-up already set out. He didn't complain. It was wonderful just to sit there while she rubbed stuff into his face then dabbed on the powder. And there was no Dodo this time. Kirsty was all on her own.

'How do I look?' he asked.

'Much better.'

'I could hardly be any worse.'

'There,' she said, standing back. 'All finished.'

'Got a mirror?'

'Right here, Gordy.'

She took the mirror from her bag and handed it to him. He was amazed! In the space of fifteen minutes, Kirsty had transformed him – the bruises had been cleverly hidden by foundation, but the make-up didn't look obvious.

'Well?' she said.

'I'm a new man, Kirsty.' He kissed her and peered in the mirror again. 'This is amazing. Nobody could ever tell I'd got terrible bruises.'

'It won't last too long,' she warned. 'You'll need to put more make-up on from time to time. Or get one of the girls at your house to do it for you.'

'Suzie – she volunteered.' He handed the

mirror back. 'That's made all the difference, Kirst. Now I'm going after those thugs who attacked us. Particularly the one who clobbered me with that pole. I was a bit embarrassed about being seen in public with a battered face. But it's fine now.'

'But we wouldn't know where to start, Gordy.'

'Along the route of the march. That's where they'll be. We're going to play at being detectives. Will you come with me?'

'Of course. Anything to catch those hooligans.'

'What are we waiting for, then?' he said, clapping his hands together. 'Let's get straight over there.'

'We'll have to stop at my flat first,' she said, 'to pick up Dodo. We can't leave her out.'

'I could!' said Gordy, under his breath.

'Every detective needs a bloodhound remember?'

Gordy rolled his eyes to heaven. He'd been foiled again.

—⋀—

There was no point in lying to her, Hayley deserved the truth. She'd always been a special friend so Karlene decided to tell her exactly what Zack had said.

'Sorry,' said Karlene. 'I've only made

everything worse.'

'It was my fault. I was the one who asked you to sound him out. I had no idea Zack would react like that. Well, it proves one thing, anyway.'

'What's that?'

'That there's something seriously wrong.'

'I've never known him react like that before.'

'Maybe I should just keep out of his way for a while.'

'Is that what you want to do?'

'No,' said Hayley, firmly. 'I want to grab hold of him, give him a good shake and ask him what he's playing at! But somehow I don't think that would work. He needs space to get himself sorted out.'

'Until he comes to his senses. He'd be crazy to let you go.'

Hayley grinned. 'That's the way *I* feel as well,' she said. 'Unfortunately, Zack has other ideas. Thanks anyway, Karlene.'

Hayley said goodbye. 'See you tomorrow. We'll have lunch together in the canteen.'

'OK, it's a date.'

They'd been standing near the main gate of the hospital. As Hayley left in one direction, Karlene began to walk in the other. She heard footsteps running up behind her.

'Wait for me!' called a familiar voice.

'Oh! Hi, Suzie,' she said, as her friend caught her up. 'Finished for the day?'

'Yes. I'm exhausted, Karlene.'

'My turn to make the evening meal. Is pasta OK?'

'Sounds good to me.'

'There's some of that red wine left, too.'

'That sounds even better.' They laughed. 'I saw you talking to Hayley just now.'

'Yes – she's got boyfriend trouble.'

'How well do you know Hayley?'

'As well as anyone, I suppose. Why?'

'I just wondered,' said Suzie. 'One or two odd things have been happening in the X-ray Department. Hayley's been involved and it got me thinking, that's all.'

'About what?'

'About how honest she is. Could you really *trust* her, Karlene?'

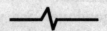

It was a small restaurant not far from the hospital. Carl and Bella were sitting at a table in an alcove. The lighting was subdued and the candle on their table threw a romantic glow over them. Bella had raced home from the Maternity Hospital to have a bath and change. Her dress was red satin and clung to her body, showing off her figure beautifully. Carl had been very struck by it when he'd first seen Bella.

'I hope you like Italian food,' he said.

'Mmm! I love it, Carl. I take my turn in the kitchen at home, and I've been trying to learn a bit more about Italian cooking.'

'Good for you. Who's making the meal tonight?'

'Karlene – that usually means pasta, too.'

'So you've swapped one Italian dish for another,' Carl joked.

'You're my dish, Carl,' said Bella, smiling.

He laughed as the waitress brought two large menus to their table. Carl ordered a bottle of wine, glanced at his menu, but Bella was much more interested in talking than eating, right now.

'What do you think your chances are,' she

asked, 'of getting the job at the hospital?'

'Who knows?' Carl shrugged.

'They ought to jump at you. I wish I could pull a few strings to help you myself.'

'No, Bella,' he said. 'No interfering, it wouldn't be right and I wouldn't want it, anyhow. What I do, I do on my own.'

'Of course,' said Bella. 'I understand that.'

'Now, what are you going to have for a starter?'

'The same as you.'

'Fettucini?'

'Suits me,' she said.

'What about a main dish?' said Carl, looking through the menu. 'Chicken, pizza, veal? What about some fish?'

'I'm easy – just order the same for both of us.'

Carl grinned and put the menu aside. 'I checked up on the boy who had the accident again today. He seemed much better. His mother had taken him a catalogue so that he could choose a new mountain bike. He'll probably be riding it in no time.'

'Let's hope he has more luck in the future.'

'Yes,' said Carl, leaning back in his chair. 'One thing, anyway – I've made up my mind about those other jobs I was thinking about.'

'As a GP?' asked Bella.

'Yes, I don't want either of them. The truth is, I realize now I don't want to go into general practice. I'd only be following in my father's footsteps and that wouldn't do me any good.'

'I think you're right, Carl.'

'Then there's the question of money,' he explained. 'You don't just become a GP and take home a fat salary every month. You have to buy into the practice, and that's very expensive. I don't have a lot of capital behind me, so they'd have to take it out of my salary each month, instead.'

'That sounds difficult,' said Bella, thoughtfully.

'It can be. A GP is like a director of a company, you're expected to invest in that company before you can earn the dividends.'

'So you'd be better off at the hospital?'

'Financially, yes. And emotionally as well,' he said, smiling into her eyes. 'City Hospital wins hands down!'

The waitress brought their wine and Carl tasted it, then nodded his approval. When she'd taken their order, the waitress went back to the kitchen and they lifted their glasses.

'Good luck in the interview!' said Bella.

'To us!' he corrected.

They clinked their glasses and sipped the wine.

'You're looking great tonight, Bella!' Bella heard an Australian voice behind her. 'What's the big occasion?'

Damian had just come into the restaurant and his handsome face was grinning broadly. Smiling at Bella, he looked inquiringly at Carl. She introduced them and they shook hands. Bella suddenly saw a chance to get some free advice for Carl.

'Damian works at the hospital, Carl – he's a doctor,' she said.

'Oh really?' said Carl.

Damian grinned again. 'Yeah, Casualty – non-stop action. I've been at it since eight this morning. You could say it's the sharp end of medicine!'

'Carl's hoping to work with us as well,' explained Bella.

'Are you?' said Damian, pleasantly.

'It's a possibility, yes. I've got an interview tomorrow.'

'Well, good luck, mate!' said Damian.

'If there's anything you want to know,' urged Bella, 'ask Damian now.'

'Sure, Carl. Any friend of Bella's is a friend of mine. She's quite something, believe me.' He shrugged. 'So, how can I help?'

'I'm not sure you can,' said Carl. He was beginning to look tense.

'Yes, I don't mind giving you some inside information, Carl. Try me!'

'I think I can manage without that, thanks,' said Carl.

'OK,' said Damian, moving away. 'I'll leave the pair of you to it. Don't want to cramp your style, mate. All the best for tomorrow!'

Damian went over to join a friend on the other side of the restaurant. Bella felt quite embarrassed. She couldn't understand why Carl had been so unfriendly to a fellow doctor. She looked at him, concerned.

'Is anything the matter, Carl?'

'I'm hungry, that's all,' he said, visibly trying to relax. He smiled suddenly, and Bella soon forgot all about Damian Holt.

They set off from exactly the same spot as before. The traffic was light, so they could walk in the road most of the time. Gordy and Kirsty were having their own private march for Animal Welfare. Dodo, the Dalmation, padded along behind them on his lead, sniffing the gutter. Gordy's face showed no sign of the bruises which were covered by make-up, and he was wearing his baseball cap pulled down low on his head as well.

As they turned into the High Street, they had to step on to the pavement, to let a double-decker bus go past.

'How would you fancy living in that, Kirst?' he said.

'What? In a bus?'

'Yes, Mark and Bella went to a party last night with some New Age travellers. Six of them live in a double-decker bus, painted every colour of the rainbow.'

'I don't think it would suit me,' she said. 'Or Dodo, for that matter.'

'Bella said it was a brilliant party.'

'Bella does seem to have some weird friends,' said Kirsty.

'It was Mark, really,' said Gordy. 'He met a girl in Maternity and she invited him to her party. She's about to have a baby but apparently she managed to dance all night!'

'That won't do the baby much good.'

Arriving at the exact spot where the attack had happened, they stopped. Just being there again made Gordy's head throb. He could almost feel the pole being smashed against his skull. His mind clouded over for a second, till Dodo's whine jerked him back to the present.

'This is exactly where it happened,' said Kirsty, pointing. 'In the struggle, we must have moved five or ten metres forwards.'

'I need to find out which direction the gang came from,' said Gordy. 'Look! Over there!'

Gordy pointed to a narrow lane off to the right. It was closed to traffic, and connected the High Street with the road parallel to it. They walked across to investigate further. It seemed an ideal place to wait in readiness for an ambush. Further down the lane, Gordy saw a pub sign swinging gently in the breeze.

'*The White Horse*. My guess is the gang met there. A couple of beers to get tanked up, then – charge! One of the guys I wrestled with had certainly been drinking – I could smell beer on his breath.'

'So *The White Horse* was their rendezvous, you think?'

'Yes, Kirst. I bet they deliberately chose a pub named after an animal – *The White Horse*. It probably seemed like a great joke to them. I can still hear them sniggering! Let's go!' he said. 'If they did use the pub on the day of the march, someone may remember them – or even know their names. We might be lucky!'

As they walked down the lane, Kirsty eyed the pub suspiciously. It looked neglected – one of the window panes was cracked and the white horse itself was badly in need of some paint.

'It looks a bit rough, Gordy,' she said, anxiously.

'Then it would have been perfect for them.'

'Do you *really* want to go in?' she asked him.

'We have to, Kirst. It's the only way we'll find out.'

Gordy pushed open the door of the lounge bar and Dodo trotted obediently beside them. The place was quite full and the customers looked round to see who the newcomers were. Before they'd even reached the bar, a voice stopped them.

'Hey!' said the barman, pointing to a big sign on the wall. 'Can't you read. No animals in here!'

'Not even a white horse?' said Gordy, cheekily.

'Very funny, mate. Now get out! All three of you!' He turned and smirked at his customers.

Dejected, they turned and trudged back into the street. Kirsty was relieved to get out but Gordy felt frustrated. Once again, Dodo had got in his way.

'You could go back in on your own,' Kirsty suggested.

'I will, tomorrow, Kirst. In daylight and without Dodo.'

It wasn't often that Karlene found herself alone in the house, but everyone else was out that evening. Bella was having dinner with Carl, Gordy was out with Kirsty and Mark was working late at the hospital. Suzie had eaten with Karlene but then she'd gone off to babysit for a neighbour. The house was quiet for once. It felt weird.

While she had the chance, Karlene decided to have a bath, but as soon as she turned on the taps, the doorbell rang. Muttering under her breath, she turned them off again, and went downstairs in her dressing gown. She was surprised to see Zack.

'Hi, Karlene. Have you got a minute?'

'Yes, of course. Come on in.'

'Not disturbing anything, am I?' he said, stepping into the living room.

'No, of course not,' said Karlene, closing the front door and joining him. Zack looked uneasy. He never found apologies very easy.

'Well, what is it, Zack?' she prompted.

'I just popped in to say sorry, that's all. For losing my temper like that and stalking out.'

'It was partly my fault, Zack. I shouldn't have poked my nose into your business.'

'That's what friends are for, isn't it? To offer help when they think you're in trouble,' said Zack, looking embarrassed.

'And are you in trouble, Zack?'

'No!' he said, smiling suddenly. 'But I will be, if I keep messing Hayley around. She won't put up with any more and I'd be crazy to lose a girl like her.'

'That's what I told you.'

'I rang her at home,' he explained. 'We had a long talk and I offered to make it up. We're going to see the late film tonight.'

'That's great! It's the best news I've had all day, Zack.'

'Hayley's meeting me at the cinema but I wanted to call in here first, to try and straighten things out with you.'

'There's nothing to straighten out,' said Karlene, kindly.

'There is, Karlene. We work together and I didn't want any tension between us in Physio. So – are we still friends?'

'Yes!' she said, giving him a friendly kiss. 'We always were!'

'Why don't you come to the movie with us? It was Hayley's idea, really. All three of us together. Come on – get your coat and we'll meet her at the cinema.'

'It's a nice idea,' said Karlene, 'but I think I'll stay here. You and Hayley go on your own.'

'Are you sure?'

'Yes, dead sure, Zack. She's been really worried about you.'

'Yes,' he sighed. 'I know.'

'You don't need me hanging around. Just enjoy the film together – and make it up with her properly. She deserves it.'

'I know she does,' agreed Zack.

But a worried look had suddenly come into his eyes.

CHAPTER NINE

Bella had never known two hours pass so quickly and so pleasurably. She'd hardly tasted the food. She was so busy listening to Carl that the meal was incidental. He talked about his life in Ireland, his time at medical school and his ambitions. There was only one thing he missed out.

'You haven't mentioned marriage.'

'We hardly know each other,' he joked.

'How would a wife fit into your plans?'

'She'd be right at the centre of them, Bella.'

'What about children?'

'Four, at least.'

'I've always wanted a large family, as well.'

'There were ten in mine. That's what *I* call large.'

'Oh,' said Bella, sitting up. 'I don't think I'd want to have that many. I'd spend all my life in the Maternity Hospital!' She laughed.

'You're far too young to think about kids yet,' he said, reaching over to hold her hand. 'You've got years of fun ahead of you first.'

'Being a nurse is not exactly fun, Carl.'

'I was thinking of your time away from the hospital.'

The waitress brought the bill and Carl paid in

cash. On their way out, they passed Damian, who was sitting with a colleague from Casualty.

'Bye, Damian,' said Bella.

'Oh, yeah. Bye, Bella. You too, Carl.'

Carl nodded at him and opened the door.

'I hope you really show them all tomorrow!' said Damian. 'They always look for confidence in a doctor,' he added, helpfully.

'Carl's got plenty of that,' said Bella, proudly.

She smiled at Damian's friend and went out into the street with Carl. His Austin Metro was parked at the kerb. As they got in, she sensed a slight uneasiness on his part.

'Anything wrong, Carl?'

'No, nothing.'

'It was Damian, wasn't it? You don't like him.'

'He's not my type, no.'

'He's a really good doctor, you know – he might have helped you.'

'I'll manage without any assistance from him.' Carl looked angry.

'Why? What have you got against Damian?'

Carl looked at her and gave her a weak smile.

'What do you think, Bella?'

'You're not *jealous*, are you?'

'He was just too familiar, that's all.'

'But Australians are always like that,' laughed Bella.

'But his one happens to be an old boyfriend of yours.'

'That's all in the past,' she assured him. 'Damian's no competition for you, Carl. He's really immature.'

'I didn't like the way he grinned at you.'

'He looks at every girl like that, silly. It doesn't mean anything. The point is, I don't fancy Damian.'

'You did once – you admitted it.'

'That was *ages* ago. Look, take me home,' she said, quietly, 'and I'll show you why I prefer Dr Carl Mullen to a hundred Dr Damian Holts.'

He started the car and drove Bella back to her road, parking some distance from the house so that they weren't under the glare of a street light. As his headlights died, they were alone in the darkness. Bella leant her head against his shoulder.

'Why don't you come into the house?' she whispered.

'Better not.'

'They've all gone to bed. We could be alone downstairs. Or we can go up to my room, if you like.'

'No, Bella, that would be even worse.'

'Why don't you take me back to your hotel, then?'

'I'd like to,' he said, 'but we aren't allowed to

have guests in our rooms. There's a night porter and he'd be sure to see us sneaking in. Besides, I need my beauty sleep tonight.'

'Don't you *want* us to be together?' Bella asked.

'Of course. But there's the interview tomorrow.'

'Yes, I'd forgotten that.'

'Well, I haven't. I'd love to spend more time with you, but I can hardly turn up at an important interview with bags under my eyes. Who'd want to appoint a doctor who yawns all over everyone?'

'You're right, sorry, Carl. I shouldn't have kept you out this late.'

'It's been a fantastic evening.'

'Thanks for asking me.'

He kissed Bella and stroked her cheek. When he spoke next, there was a note of envy in his voice.

'Are you sure you prefer me to Damian Holt?'

'Never heard of him,' said Bella, slipping both her arms around Carl. 'Who wants an old flame when I can have a roaring bonfire? Come here!'

She kissed him with such passion that Carl's jealousy vanished completely. Bella was floating on air!

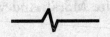

Mark arrived at the Maternity Hospital next morning and was met by a surprise. Jasmine was sitting alone in the reception area, looking frightened and worried. There was no sign of her smiling face and girlish giggle. All she could manage was a small wave.

'Good morning, Jasmine,' he said.

'Hi, Mark.'

'What's the problem?'

'There isn't one,' she said, looking relieved. 'It was a false alarm. I thought the baby was coming and got into a real panic. It was scary. I didn't know what to do.'

'You should get here as fast as possible, Jasmine.'

'But *how*? I was stuck in the bus on my own. Baz and Raphael have got part-time jobs, so have the girls. People think we're spongers, but we always get some sort of work wherever we stop. We need money, just like anybody else. Especially with the baby coming.'

'Why didn't you phone for a taxi?'

'That's what I did,' she said. 'Eventually. But I had to stagger a couple of hundred metres to the nearest phone box. I didn't think I was going to make it, honestly.'

'Haven't you got a phone of your own?'

'In a bus? No, Mark. And we can't afford a

mobile. I was stuck and it really frightened me, I can tell you! In the end, I got a taxi to rush me here and it was a false alarm.'

'But I bet the alarm wasn't false to you,' said Mark, sympathetically. 'You must have been in a terrible state.'

'I felt hysterical and I still feel jumpy. That's why I'm sitting here. I'm not moving out of this hospital until I feel calmer and get my strength back.' Jasmine shuddered. 'I really thought I was about to give birth in the taxi.'

'You should ring for an ambulance next time.'

'Would they come?' Jasmine looked surprised.

'Of course!' said Mark. 'It's an emergency. Paramedics are trained in midwifery as well, just in case. Dial 999 and ask for Hospital Services. An ambulance would get to you quicker than a taxi.'

'I never thought of that, I was in such a panic.' She took several deep breaths to try and calm herself.

'Anyway,' she said, 'I was lucky. I'm well, and the baby's healthy, so I must be grateful.' She gave him a tired smile. 'Sorry to let it out at you, Mark. How are you, anyway?'

'I'm fine, Jasmine.'

'Where's Bella today?'

'Don't ask! She had a late night and couldn't

wake up this morning. She sent me on ahead so at least one of us could get here on time!'

'Did she enjoy our party?'

'Yes, we both did. It was great.'

'Bella was a big hit. Raphael really fancied her, I think. So did Baz, too.' She laughed.

'They'll have to wait their turn in the queue,' said Mark, shaking his head and smiling.

'She told me about this doctor she's met. Carl something? What's he like?' asked Jasmine.

'None of us have met him yet. Bella's keeping him to herself. But I can tell you one thing, Jasmine – it's serious.'

Jasmine started to giggle and Mark felt reassured. She was beginning to get some of her old spirit back. He hated the idea of her being so distressed, she was such a warm and friendly person. Mark began to think how he could help her.

———∧———

Gordy sat on the bench while Kirsty studied his face carefully. He was giving up his lunch hour to rush back to *The White Horse* and she was checking to see if his bruises were properly disguised by the make-up.

'That's better than I could do it, Gordy,' she said.

'Suzie's been helping me.'

'She did a good job.'

'I know and it means I can actually look in a mirror without being scared out of my wits!'

'Your face was never that bad,' said Kirsty, laughing.

'I'd better get going. Wish me good luck.'

'Take care,' she said, kissing him. 'I want you back in one piece.'

'Don't worry, I'll be fine.'

They'd been in the garden behind the hospital, and now Gordy let himself out and started to head towards the High Street. As he turned into the lane with the pub, he stopped to check his reflection in a shop window. No bruises were visible. He pulled his baseball cap down over his forehead and walked towards the pub.

The bar was fairly busy and he had to wait before he could be served. He looked around to see if he could spot either of the two youths who'd attacked him during the riot – but they didn't seem to be there. The barman was the same one who'd been on duty the night before, a big, stocky man in his fifties, with tattoos on his forearms. Eventually, he turned to Gordy.

'What can I get you, mate?' he said.

'Half of lager, please.'

'Anything else?'

'And one of those ham rolls.'

'Right-o, coming up.'

Gordy was still searching the faces around the room as he paid the barman and took a sip of his lager.

'Looking for someone?' asked the man.

'Yeah,' said Gordy. 'Two guys who were in here the day of that march; the one that ended in a riot.'

The barman's eyes narrowed with suspicion. 'You're not a copper, are you?'

'No way!'

'You sure? We don't like coppers in here.'

'I'm a medical student,' said Gordy.

The man relaxed. 'That's all right, then. So, who are these two blokes? There was a whole crowd of them in here that day.'

'I knew it!' said Gordy under his breath.

'They sat round boozing for a couple of hours,' the barman went on, 'then this geezer sticks his head through the door and says "They're coming, lads! Let's go!" Then they all charges out.'

'So they weren't regulars, then?'

'No, mate. A couple of them come in 'ere from time to time, but I've never set eyes on most of 'em. But they can come again, if they like. Drank lots of beer – good for business, that was.'

'And you recognized a couple of them?' asked Gordy.

'Yeah. One's called Jacko, the other's Phil.'

'Where do they come from, do you know?'

'That's all I can tell you, mate. I just serve the booze here, I don't get a life story off every customer. But they usually come in of an evening.'

'Thanks,' said Gordy. 'You've been a big help. Let me buy you a drink. What'll you have?'

'A pint, thanks.' The barman grinned. 'That proves it, then. You're definitely not a copper. You won't find one of them buying someone a drink. They're mean devils.'

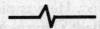

Bella sprinted across the hospital car park, dodging the lines of vehicles. By the time she reached the main block, she was out of breath. She pushed open the main door and went through into Reception. Carl wasn't there. She stamped her foot in frustration. She was about to go on up to the canteen, when he came out of the shop, carrying a newspaper. Relieved, she dashed over to him.

'Thought I'd missed you!' she said.

'I was just about to go on up, Bella. I bought a paper to read in case there's a long, nervous wait.' He grinned.

'It'll be long and nervous for me, Carl. Look, I'm sorry I'm late, the Ward Sister made me work an extra half-hour because I was late getting here this morning.'

'That was my fault,' he said with a smile.

'I'm not complaining. How do you feel, Carl?'

'Quite confident, really,' he said.

'Go in there with both guns blazing!'

'That's not my style, Bella. I'll just play it cool.'

'Lots of luck, anyway,' she said, kissing him. 'I'm glad I got here in time to see you before the interview.'

They were still gazing into each other's eyes when Mark arrived. He was pleased he had the chance to meet Bella's mysterious boyfriend at last.

'Hello,' he said.

'Oh, Mark,' said Bella, 'this is Doctor Carl Mullen.'

Mark and Carl shook hands politely.

'I've told you about Mark,' she said.

'Yes,' said Carl, moving away. 'Nice to meet you, Mark. Sorry I can't stop – I've got an interview for a job. Must go.'

He ran up the stairs with Bella waving at him. Mark was puzzled. Why had Carl left so fast? It was almost as if he was afraid of something.

CHAPTER TEN

Wearing her uniform, Suzie came into the waiting room of the X-ray Department and looked around at the patients.

'Dennis Reynolds?' she asked.

'That's me,' said a man to her left.

'Would you put this on, please?' she said, handing him a loose, cotton gown. 'You can use the first cubicle.'

'Right. Thanks.'

'When you're ready, just take a seat again.'

Reynolds nodded and went into the cubicle. He was a middle-aged man in a brown suit, short, balding and fidgety. Suzie could smell tobacco smoke on his clothes when he stood too close. He was obviously a heavy smoker.

Another patient emerged from one of the X-ray rooms and the radiographer popped her head out.

'Next, please!' called Joan Cross.

'Mrs Angela Larraby,' said Suzie, reading from her list, 'could you go in with Mrs Cross, please?'

The patient, dressed in the standard hospital gown, tied at the back, went in to have her X-ray. Suzie followed her, closing the door behind them.

'Hello, Mrs Larraby,' said Joan, smiling. 'Just lie on here for me, please, and we'll have you finished in no time.'

'Thank you,' said the patient, settling down on the bed.

'And don't look so worried. It's quite painless. We haven't lost a patient yet, have we, Suzie? Now, are you quite comfortable down there?'

Suzie liked working with Joan Cross. She was a chatty woman in her thirties with a northern accent. Some of the radiographers were rather brisk with the patients, but Joan always had a smile and a cheery word. Her X-rays were of a high quality and Suzie had learnt a lot from watching her.

Soon, another patient was leaving the room.

'Next, please,' said Joan. 'Who is it, Suzie?'

'Dennis Reynolds. For a chest X-ray.'

'Shoot him straight in. Then you can take your break.'

'Don't you want me to help?'

'No, thanks. I can do chest X-rays with my eyes closed. You've worked hard, have a rest. Oh, and tell Hayley I'd like to see her. She's supposed to put all these X-rays in the storage unit. They're mounting up. Where is she? I haven't seen her anywhere. She must've wandered off somewhere. Hayley's getting so scatterbrained these days.'

Zack was at his best in the gymnasium that afternoon. He worked patiently with Lisa until the little girl was moving her injured arm with much greater ease. Zack slipped her a small bag of jelly babies as a reward. Lisa was delighted as she went off to her mother.

Karlene had been watching her friend in action. 'You've got Lisa eating out of your hand, Zack.'

'Yes,' he said. 'Eating jelly babies!'

'Thank you for last night. It meant a lot to me,' said Karlene. 'It really cleared the air and I'm very grateful.'

'I didn't want us to have a misunderstanding, that's all.'

'We won't now. How was the film?'

'The film was a waste of time, to be honest,' Zack said, shaking his head.

'Just as well I missed it, then.'

'Hayley and I crept out halfway through. We decided to go to a café nearby.'

'You probably needed time for a real chat.'

Zack grunted. They were tidying away some of the equipment they'd used with patients in the gymnasium. Karlene was remembering a remark that Suzie had made to her about

Hayley. It had made Karlene uneasy. She was certain her friend was trustworthy.

'Does Hayley like being in the X-ray Department?' she asked.

'As far as I know she does,' said Zack.

'Doesn't she talk about her work much?'

'Not usually, no.'

'What about you?' said Karlene. 'Do you discuss the Physio Department with her?'

'Sometimes, yes.'

'I just wondered if she was happy over there, that's all.'

'Why don't you ask Hayley yourself?'

'But I'd like to hear what you think, Zack.'

'I don't know, really.'

'But Hayley's your girlfriend,' reminded Karlene. 'Don't you mind if she's enjoying her work or not?'

'Look,' said Zack, turning to face her. 'You might as well hear it from me, before Hayley tells you yourself. Things just didn't work out last night. We had a big row at the cinema. That's why we walked out of the film.'

'Oh,I see.'

'We decided to split up for good.'

'That's terrible!' said Karlene. She could see the hurt in Zack's eyes. 'Was it your idea or Hayley's?'

'Mine. We won't be seeing each other again,' he said, and he walked away, quickly.

———⋀———

Bella couldn't wait to leave the Maternity Hospital at the end of the afternoon. As she and Mark were making up a bed in a side-ward, she kept checking her watch.

'Relax,' said Mark. 'Carl will wait for you.'

'I can't bear the suspense.'

'How do you think he'll get on in the interview?'

'He'll be brilliant,' said Bella. 'I've never met anyone who knows as much about medicine as Carl. And he's so poised and confident.'

'He wasn't very poised when I met him earlier. One look at me, and he ran away at once.'

'He had to get to his interview, Mark. I'd held him up long enough as it was. It was nothing to do with you. What did you think of him, anyway?'

'He's exactly as you described him, Bella.'

'Tall, handsome and all mine!' she said, laughing.

They finished making the bed and straightened up. Bella glanced at her watch again – she still had five minutes to wait before she could rush off.

'You missed Jasmine this morning,' said Mark. 'What was she doing here?'

'She thought she was having the baby.'

'Did she go into labour?'

'No, it was a false alarm, Bella. But she looked very shaken. She'd been stuck on her own in that bus, not able to call a taxi or an ambulance. Apparently, the rest of them had all gone out to work. It was all she could do to stagger down to the phone box. I can see why she was so anxious. She's completely isolated there.'

'Poor girl! What a position to be in!' Bella thought for a moment then snapped her fingers. 'I've got it!'

'What?'

'Suzie! She's the answer to Jasmine's problem. Her parents gave her a mobile phone for Christmas, but she hardly ever uses it.'

'It's too expensive, that's why.'

'But we could ask her to lend it to Jasmine.'

'That's a brilliant idea, Bella!'

'It would only be for a short while - a week or two at most.' Bella grinned. 'Even less if Jasmine carries on dancing like she did at the party. What do you think, Mark?'

'I'll speak to Suzie tonight.'

'Oops! Time to go. Keep your fingers crossed for Carl.'

'He's bound to get the job, Bella. If he's half as good as you say he is, they'll put him in charge of the whole hospital. Go on, off you go!'

Bella flew out of the Maternity Hospital as if she had wings on her heels. She ran straight across to the main block. Carl had promised to meet her there, at the end of the afternoon. But there was no trace of him. She looked in the shop this time, but he wasn't in there. Bella was puzzled. The interviews couldn't still be going on, that would mean they'd have lasted over three hours!

She paced restlessly up and down in Reception until one of the lifts opened. It had a full load. As the people got out, Bella stepped forward, hoping that Carl would be among them – but he wasn't. It was infuriating! After another five minutes of waiting, she couldn't stand it any more. She pressed the lift button herself and went up to the first floor.

Hospital Management occupied a suite of offices at the far end of the main corridor. Bella had taken Carl there on her tour of the building. She'd even shown him into the boardroom, where interviews always took place. It had given him some idea of what he was about to face. As she walked along the corridor, some of the clerical staff were leaving.

Bella went up to one of them. 'Have the interviews finished yet?' she asked.

'What interviews? We haven't had any

interviews up here today,' said the girl. 'The boardroom's locked up.'

'It can't be!'

'It is, I'm afraid. See for yourself.'

Bella was mortified. What was going on?

———◆———

Suzie spent the whole afternoon helping Joan Cross in the X-ray Department. It wasn't until she was leaving that she finally had the chance of a quiet word with Hayley. They were in the little staff room. Hayley seemed more down and distracted than ever.

'What's the problem, Hayley?' she asked.

'It's Zack. It's all off. I thought everything would be fine when he rang me yesterday.'

'Yes,' said Suzie. 'Karlene told me he was taking you to the cinema. Zack called at the house on his way. I thought he was talking about making it up with you.'

'That was the idea, Suzie.'

'So what happened?'

'I don't know. I must've said the wrong thing. Zack suddenly began shouting at me, in the middle of the film.'

'What did you do?'

'Shouted back, of course,' said Hayley, defiantly. 'Nobody pushes me around, not even

114

Zack. When he stormed out, I went after him and we had a real argument in the foyer. It got a bit heated and they asked us to leave in the end.'

Hayley shrugged philosophically. 'It's over, Suzie. It was great while it lasted, but I'm not putting up with that kind of stuff. Zack Hilliard is no more!'

She waved goodbye to Suzie as she went out. Suzie felt very sad. Zack and Hayley had seemed such a happy couple. She began to wonder what really lay behind the split.

Catherine White came into the staffroom with a clipboard.

'Ah, Suzie,' she said. 'I'm glad I've caught you. Another set of X-rays is missing.'

'I don't believe it!'

'Well, they're not in the storage unit. I've just searched.'

'Who's the patient?'

'Dennis Reynolds.'

'I remember him,' said Suzie. 'Joan Cross took the X-rays but she couldn't find Hayley. She asked me to put the set into the storage unit. They're bound to be there.'

'Then I'd be very grateful if you could find them.'

'I will, Catherine. Wait here.'

Suzie left the staffroom swiftly and went

straight to the storage unit. She was about to open the door when she heard a noise inside. Inching forward, she peered through the glass panel in the door. What she saw made her gasp. Hayley was there, searching through the racks of X-rays.

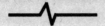

CHAPTER ELEVEN

Suzie was in a predicament. She wasn't sure if she ought to barge into the storage unit and challenge Hayley then and there, or just walk in and pretend to be surprised when she saw her. Hayley shouldn't have been in there at all. Sets of X-rays were supposed to be kept under lock and key, until they were needed. Under no circumstances could anyone take them out of the hospital.

Hayley was acting strangely, but she was still Suzie's friend and colleague and she deserved the chance to explain herself. Suzie decided not to jump on her as if she'd caught her in the act of stealing X-rays. A more tactful approach was needed. She pushed open the door and Hayley looked up, guiltily, but recovered very quickly.

'Hi, Suzie,' she said.

'I thought you'd gone home,' said Suzie.

'I was just going. I was doing a bit of tidying up,' said Hayley. 'The bust-up with Zack last night really got to me. I've been wandering around in a daze, making all kinds of stupid mistakes. I even had Joan Cross yelling at me!'

'She couldn't find you when she needed you, that's why.'

'I was probably in the Ladies having a good cry.'

'Is it that bad?' asked Suzie, kindly.

Hayley nodded. 'I really loved him, Suzie. I still do.'

'Did you tell him that last night?'

'I didn't get the chance.' She stood back from the racks. 'Anyway, I just popped in to check that everything was in order. I'd put three sets of X-rays in the wrong place this morning.'

'Were they today's batch? Only I wanted the ones belonging to a Dennis Reynolds.'

'I don't remember bringing those in.'

'No,' said Suzie. 'Joan gave them to me because you'd disappeared somewhere. And I put them right here.' She took out a set of X-rays. 'There you are. Mr Reynolds. Exactly where I left them.'

'Your eyesight's getting better, Suzie.'

'Catherine White wants them.'

'I'll go before she sees me. Joan threatened to complain to her if I didn't get myself sorted out. I must go, I'm meeting Karlene in the canteen.'

'See you tomorrow then, Hayley. Bye.'

But Suzie wasn't entirely convinced by her excuse. Why hadn't Hayley come in earlier to make sure that everything was in order? Suzie was thoughtful. She ran her finger along the rack, wondering if her friend was telling the truth or not. The door opened and Catherine White popped her head in.

'Any luck?'

'They were here all the time, Catherine.'

'In today's batch?'

'Yes,' said Suzie.

'Well, they weren't there five minutes ago,' said her tutor, taking them from Suzie. 'Somebody must have come in here and put them back.'

Suzie began to have second thoughts about Hayley.

Bella felt utterly dejected. Her whole world seemed to have shattered before her eyes. She'd placed such faith in Carl that it never occurred to her that he might be lying. No interviews had taken place in the boardroom that afternoon – Bella was certain of that. Carl had been having her on. She felt such a fool for trusting him so completely.

Feeling utterly hopeless, she went back downstairs to Reception. She was too upset to go home yet. She'd only have to face a series of embarrassing questions from her friends. She knew that Mark had doubts about Carl and it looked as though he'd been right. But it was a painful thing to admit to herself.

She suddenly felt exhausted and, seeing an empty chair in a quiet corner, she went over and flopped into it. She needed to be alone with her thoughts for a while, before she could talk to anyone. There were a lot of serious questions that she had to put to herself first.

She heard someone approach, but she did not even have the heart to look up.

'Thank goodness I've found you, Bella!' he said. It was Carl, smiling down at her as calm as you please.

'What on earth are you playing at?' she demanded.

'Bella! Calm down!'

'There weren't any interviews this afternoon, Carl. I went up to the boardroom and it was locked.'

'The interviews weren't held there, after all,' he explained. 'The four of us were taken along to an office on the second floor. *That's* where we were interviewed.'

'I don't believe you,' she said, coldly.

'I swear it, Bella,' said Carl, sitting beside her and putting an arm round her shoulders. 'They only gave us fifteen minutes each, so I was finished by three o'clock. I went out to do some shopping and was a bit late getting back, that's all.'

Bella was still suspicious. 'Is this true, Carl?'

'On my word of honour.'

'And you really are a doctor?'

'Bella!' Her accusation made him wince. 'After all I've told you about myself, how can you say a thing like that? I'm shocked.' He looked annoyed as he opened his briefcase. 'If you want written proof, you can have it. I had to produce all this at the interview.' He took out a folder. 'Here! Take it, Bella. Go on. They're all there. All my credentials.'

Bella looked sheepish as she opened the folder. She looked down at a large certificate from a medical school in Dublin. It told her that Doctor Carl Mullen had been awarded a degree and was now a Bachelor of Medicine. Bella felt more uncomfortable than ever. He pointed to the sheaf of papers underneath the certificate.

'Read them all!' he urged. 'References, letters from my professors – they're all perfectly genuine.'

'I can see that,' she said, meekly. 'Here, have them back.'

'Thanks.' He put them into the briefcase and snapped it shut. 'This has really upset me, Bella. I thought we were friends.'

'We are, Carl!'

'Not if you're going to call me a liar.'

'I take it back,' she said, quickly. 'Try and see it

from my point of view. It all seemed to click into place.'

'What did, Bella?'

'Don't stare at me like that, Carl. It frightens me!'

'Sorry.' Carl made an effort to calm down and took hold of her hand. 'Tell me the truth. What *did* you think?'

'That maybe you'd made it all up,' she said. 'You were so weird when you met Damian, and then it was the same with Mark. You just didn't seem to want to talk to them. Then there was all that mystery about your hotel. Why wouldn't you tell me where it was?'

'Because I was too ashamed, Bella. It was so small and sleazy but it's all I could afford. I haven't got any income. I had to scrimp and save to get the money to come over here. Was there anything else that bothered you?'

'Well... your car.'

'What was wrong with it?'

'Nothing,' she said, 'except that it's too old to be a hire car. And if you're short of cash, you couldn't have bought one in the short time you've been here. So where did that Metro come from?'

'My brother, Liam. My younger brother.'

'You never told me about him.'

'I never told you about my three sisters and my

122

other brothers, either, but it doesn't mean they don't exist. Liam's at art college over here. He said I could borrow his old banger for a week or two, until I found my feet. Any more accusations?'

'No, no, nothing.' Bella looked sad. 'I didn't mean to doubt you, Carl. Please, don't be angry with me.'

'I won't,' he promised. 'Anyway, it suits you. That egg on your face makes you look even lovelier.'

He kissed her cheek and she began to cry. She was so relieved that she hadn't driven him away and that he was exactly the man she believed him to be.

'Aren't you forgetting something?' he said. 'The interview.'

'Yes!' gasped Bella. 'How did it go?'

'Very well. They offered me the post.

'That's incredible!'

'There's only one snag, Bella. I'm not sure that I want to accept it.'

———— ⋀ ————

Hayley stared into her coffee as she stirred it. She was sitting opposite Karlene in the hospital canteen but it was a full minute before she spoke.

'What did Zack say to you?' asked Hayley.

'Very little,' replied Karlene. 'He told me that

you'd had a big row in the cinema and decided to finish with each other.'

'*He* decided that. Not me. That's the dreadful thing: I don't know why, really. In the heat of the moment, we both yelled stupid things at each other. But I still don't know exactly why Zack's gone off me.'

'I'm sure he hasn't, Hayley.'

'Then why did we have that terrible argument?'

'Why did he invite you out in the first place?'

Hayley looked down. That was the one positive thing that had happened between her and her boyfriend lately. Zack had really tried. He knew that he'd been upsetting her and he'd tried to make it up. She was trying to remember now – had it been her fault that the quarrel had started in the cinema? She went over everything in her mind.

'I didn't like the film,' she said.

'Is that why he got angry?'

'I didn't want to go to a film in the first place, Karlene. We were supposed to be getting things together again and a cinema's not exactly the best place for that. I wanted him to come back to my flat, so we could talk and be on our own.'

'I'd have wanted the same thing. So what did Zack say?'

'He just refused.'

'Did he give a reason?'

'He didn't need to,' sighed Karlene. 'I could hear it in his voice. He's gone off me completely.'

'I just don't believe that!'

'You weren't at the cinema, Karlene.'

'Maybe I should've been,' she said. 'I could have acted as a referee when you two started fighting. Then I could have banged both your heads together.'

Hayley smiled and put a hand on her arm. Karlene always took a practical view of things. Hayley was thankful that she had a friend she could talk to.

'It's not as simple as that, Karlene. There's no spark between us any more.'

'It sounds to me as if you had too many sparks flying!'

'We both lost our tempers. That wouldn't have happened if we'd been together in my flat. We could have talked *properly.* You know what I mean.' She shook her head slowly. 'It was almost as if Zack didn't want to be alone with me.'

'He does. I'm sure he does.'

Tears began to stream down Hayley's face. 'What am I going to *do*, Karlene?'

Gordy sat in the corner of the lounge bar at *The*

White Horse pub and finished his drink. It was his second pint of lager and he'd drunk both of them very slowly. He decided that he would have one more. Crossing to the bar, he ordered another one.

'How often do they come in?' asked Gordy. 'You know, those two lads you mentioned - Jacko and Phil.'

'Every once in a while.'

'When was the last time?'

'About a week ago – not counting the day of the riot, that is.'

When the lager was poured, Gordy paid for it and returned to his seat. He'd brought a newspaper so he had something to read – it was also a shield to hide behind. The bruising on his face had faded a lot and he hadn't needed much make-up. Nobody seemed to take any notice of him.

Eventually, two youths came into the pub and sauntered across to the bar. They *looked* like the thugs who'd attacked Gordy, but he couldn't be sure until he was able to catch the barman's eye for confirmation. They bought themselves a pint of beer each and sat at a table quite near Gordy. By leaning forward, he could overhear them.

'Cheers!' said one, raising his glass.

'Yeah,' said his friend.

They both drank and one of them belched

loudly. 'Remember the last time we were in here, Phil?'

'The day they had that protest march.'

'Animal Flipping Welfare!'

'We soon sorted them out, Jacko.'

They laughed coarsely and now Gordy was quite certain. It definitely was them.

CHAPTER TWELVE

After running home to change, Bella met him at the wine bar. This time, Carl was in casual clothes and he looked lean and athletic. Bella admired his broad shoulders, but without his suit he'd lost some of his authority, and Bella couldn't understand why.

They sat at a table, sharing a bottle of white wine.

'You must take the job, Carl!' she insisted.

'Don't rush me, Bella.'

'But it's exactly what you wanted,' she insisted.

'Yes and no,' he said.

'I thought you'd leap at it. So what's stopping you?' She touched his arm. 'Don't you want to be near me any more?'

'Of course I do, Bella.'

'Then accept that post at City Hospital.'

'It needs thinking about, that's all.'

'I've just thought about it for you. Take it!'

Carl dissolved into laughter. Bella could be very persuasive when she really put her mind to it. He sipped his wine and looked at her admiringly.

'Do you know the hours they work in Casualty?' he asked.

'Yes. Damian's told me. I know that they're long, tiring and very unsocial.'

'And I'd be on nights part of the time.'

'I'll sneak in to be with you,' said Bella, snuggling up to Carl. 'Or I'll injure myself, so that they'll rush me to Casualty and I can be your patient.' She punched him, playfully. 'I just want to be near you, Carl. Please – take the job!'

'When I've weighed up all the considerations.'

Bella made a face and he laughed. They were just enjoying being with each other again. All Bella's suspicions had gone. Her only concern now was to convince him to work in the same hospital as her.

'I thought you came to England to get a job, Carl. So take the only one on offer.'

'What do you mean?'

'Well, you don't like the idea of being a GP. That leaves only one possibility – City Hospital!'

'*Two* possibilities,' he corrected.

'Where's the other one?'

'St Catherine's.'

'But that's *miles* away!'

'It's not far to drive,' he argued. 'I'd buy myself a decent car. Liam's Metro's on its last legs.'

'But I don't want you to go to St Catherine's.'

'They haven't even offered me a post yet.'

'Then how is it a possibility?'

'I've been short-listed, that's all. I was keeping it as a surprise, Bella. A sort of back-up, in case the City Hospital job fell through. It would offer me something I can't get here.'

'You can't get *me* at St Catherine's.' She punched him again. 'What is this stupid job you're interested in?'

'It's a research post.'

'But you said you wanted to work with patients.'

'I will – indirectly. It's linked to their Children's Ward. I'd be doing research into a rare blood disease that affects hundreds of kids every year.' He looked serious. 'This is important work, Bella. I'd be working towards finding a cure – helping to save lives.'

'Stay here and save my life!' she cried.

'I couldn't miss an opportunity like this. It could lead to a PhD which would put me on the fast track. At the very least I ought to see what St Catherine's is like.'

Bella went very quiet. She'd been to St Catherine's. It was bigger and more modern than City Hospital. Far more money was pumped into it and its research laboratories had a good reputation. Carl was a dedicated doctor. If it was a choice between his career and her, she knew which he would choose.

'When is the interview?' she murmured.

'Next Monday.'

'What about the post at City Hospital?'

'I said I'd let them know by Tuesday.'

'Are you going to keep me on tenterhooks all weekend?'

'I have to explore every avenue, Bella.'

'But I want you here!'

'St Catherine's is not *that* far away.'

'They've got their own College of Nurses,' she moaned. 'Why drive all the way back here when you can find plenty of girls there?'

He kissed her reassuringly and refilled her glass. Bella took a long sip and tried to cheer herself up.

'I'm going to enjoy you while I've got you, then.'

'Oh, I'll be around for some time yet.'

'You'd better be!' she warned. 'Now, tell me something about Dublin?'

'It's a fine old city.'

'I've never been to Ireland. Will you take me there one day? I could meet all your brothers and sisters.'

'Oh, I wouldn't take you to Dublin, Bella. We'd go somewhere more romantic than that – Killarney, for instance, or Cork – or Waterford. You'd love them.'

'And your brother? Liam lives in England, doesn't he? I'd like to meet him some time. Where does he live?'

'Some grubby digs on the other side of the city.'

'Is he anything like you?'

'Not really, no.'

'You're the brains and Liam's the artist, is that it?'

'Something like that, Bella.' He picked up the menu. 'I'm hungry. What shall I order for you?'

'Doctor Carl Mullen at City Hospital.'

'Grilled or roasted?' joked Carl. He smiled again, but there was something different about him now. Bella couldn't quite put her finger on what it was.

───────∧───────

Mark didn't manage to get to the bus until mid-evening, when the light was starting to fade. He was surprised to find Raphael on a ladder, cleaning the top floor windows. Drizzle was falling, but it didn't seem to bother the young Spaniard. With a cigarette between his lips, he worked away methodically.

'Hello, Raphael,' called Mark. 'Is Jasmine here?'

'Si, she's inside.'

'Can I go on in?'

'Sure. Is good to see you again.'

Mark climbed into the bus and rang the conductor's bell. Jasmine's voice came from behind the thick curtain.

'Come in, come in, whoever you are!'

He went into the lower deck of the bus and found her stretched out on a sofa. She smiled at him warmly and beckoned him over for a kiss.

'Mark! What a lovely surprise!' she said.

'How are you, Jasmine?'

'Much better, thanks.'

'No more false alarms?'

'Not yet. Take a seat.'

Mark glanced around the interior. The party had been held in the half-dark, so he hadn't been able to appreciate the decor. Like the exterior, the inside had been painted in bright colours. Rugs and old carpets covered the floor and there was a mass of armchairs, sofas and stools along both walls. There was even a tiny television set with an indoor aerial. Jasmine had been watching *The Bill*.

She switched it off with the remote control. 'What brings you out here?' she asked.

'I've got a present for you,' he said. 'It's more of a loan, really – from Suzie.'

'Is she the radiographer you told me about?'

'Yes, that's right,' said Mark. 'Her parents

bought her a mobile phone for Christmas so they could keep in touch with her more easily. But Suzie hardly ever uses it.' He handed over something in a plastic bag. 'She said you could borrow it until the baby comes along.'

'Oh, that's so kind, Mark!'

'You won't have to crawl to the phone box now,' he said, smiling at her.

'No. This is a real lifeline.'

'It's easy to use – look, the instruction book's in the bag with the phone. There's only one catch...'

'What's that?'

'It's strictly for an emergency call,' warned Mark. 'Suzie doesn't want vast phone bills. The phone's only for you to use, Jasmine.'

'Nobody else will touch it, I promise! Let me make a note of your number, Mark.'

'Dial 999. That's all you need to do.'

'I want your home number, as well,' insisted Jasmine, as she reached for her handbag. 'When the time comes, I want you to be the first to know.'

'OK. Got something to write with?'

'Yes,' she said, taking out a pen and a scrap of paper. 'Give me the number, and remind me of the names of all your friends. I know Bella, who are the others?'

Mark was talking happily about his friends at the house, when the bus shook as someone came aboard. Raphael came in with a couple of cans of beer and handed one to Mark.

'Cheers!' he said. 'To my baby!'

'I'll drink to that,' said Mark.

Jasmine giggled. 'So would Baz!'

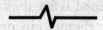

'Are you absolutely certain it was them, Gordy?' she said.

'Yes, Kirst. They were talking about the riot.'

'Didn't they recognize you?'

'I was hidden behind a newspaper,' said Gordy. 'But they wouldn't have known me, anyway. I had old clothes on for the march. I look very different in these.'

Kirsty agreed. The bright green jacket and the gaudy tie were much more typical of Gordy. It was very unlikely he would be recognized by the youths who'd sabotaged the protest march.

'You're so brave to go in there alone.'

'I did it for you, Kirst. Animal Welfare is so important to you,' he explained. 'I want to find out why they wrecked the march before I hand them over. Once the police have got them, they won't try to bring any false charges against you.'

'I'm terrified that they'll take me to court.'

'Not while I'm around.'

'You're such a comfort to me, Gordy.'

She kissed him impulsively. She'd invited Gordy to her flat at last. Dodo was shut in the bedroom and they had the sofa all to themselves.

'I'm going back tomorrow, with a tape-recorder, just in case Jacko and Phil come in again. I'll be able to record what they say and use it as evidence against them.' He pretended to look furtive. 'It's what the police do when they're working undercover. Detective-Sergeant Robbins of the CID. That's me, Kirst. I always get my man.'

Kirsty smiled happily and put her head on his shoulder. She was a serious girl who was completely committed to Animal Welfare, but she liked her pleasures as well. Gordy was determined that this was one of those moments, so he began to stroke her back.

'I'll watch that video recording again,' he said. 'Jacko and Phil will be in it.'

'Which one hit you with the pole?'

'Jacko. He was boasting about it tonight. He said he wished he'd hit me harder.'

'Poor Gordy!' she breathed. 'Does your head still hurt?'

'Yes,' he lied. 'It's pounding right now.'

'Put your head in my lap.'

Gordy rested the side of his head on her lap so that she could run her fingers gently through his hair. It was wonderful. Gordy could have stayed there all night. Kirsty's touch was so amazing. The march might have landed him in hospital but it had also brought them much closer together.

'Is that better?' she asked.

'Perfect,' sighed Gordy.

'Just close your eyes and enjoy it.'

Gordy was in heaven. He closed his eyes and felt as if he was floating on the surface of warm water. Kirsty bent over to kiss him. Then she began to lick his cheek and he groaned as he felt her hot tongue - at least he thought it was her tongue!

Suddenly, he let out a horrible yell. 'Arghhhh!'

It was Dodo, the Dalmation, licking his face. She'd got out of the bedroom and trotted over to them.

Gordy was horrified! The dog was slobbering all over him.

'You see?' said Kirsty, fondly. 'Dodo likes you!'

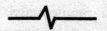

Suzie had breakfast alone that morning. She was the only person in the house who had to go to the hospital on Saturday. Because they were short-staffed in the X-ray Department, she'd volunteered to do some relief work. Suzie felt that all experience was useful, and never minded putting in some extra time. It would all be taken into account when her tutor came to write her assessment.

City Hospital was always busy on Saturdays and she had to thread her way through a crowded Reception before going to the X-ray Department. The waiting room was already filling up with patients arriving early for their appointments. Suzie went into the staffroom to change into her uniform. Joan Cross was already there. She gave Suzie a smile.

'Morning. You must love this job, Suzie.'

'I do, Joan.'

'Enjoy it while you can,' she said, 'the gloss wears off in time.'

'What do you mean exactly?'

'Well, it's all very exciting at first; helping people, being in charge of machines that cost vast amounts of money, fulfiling a key role in the hospital system.' Joan shrugged. 'After a couple of years, it's a routine job.'

'It'll never be just routine to me,' said Suzie.

'That's what I used to think, too.'

'There's so much to learn and so many different faces coming through the door every day. I never get bored.'

'I do sometimes,' admitted her tutor. 'I've been at it too long, Suzie. Maybe the stress is beginning to tell.' She laughed. 'Take no notice of me, I love the job, really. It's just a bit of a trial having to come in on a Saturday morning, when my two kids want me at home. "Why can't you be like a normal mother?" they keep asking. It's a good question and I don't have a good answer.'

'You *are* a normal mother, Joan.'

'I'm not a normal *anything*!'

'Millions of mothers go out to work.'

'Not on Saturdays.'

'Lots of women have to juggle their families and their jobs.'

'I know,' sighed Joan. 'And it's a problem. Anyway, I'm glad I've got you by my side today. We make a good team.'

'Thanks, Joan.'

'The list of patients is in Reception.'

'Shall I get the first lot changed into their gowns?'

'Please, Suzie. We start on the dot, in ten minutes.'

Suzie was rather surprised by Joan's comments. The radiographer had always seemed to take a positive attitude towards her work. It was worrying to hear her being cynical. When Suzie went into Reception, an even bigger surprise awaited her. Hayley was just arriving with a large plastic bag in her hand.

'Hayley!'

'Oh hi, Suzie.'

'You're not supposed to be in today, are you?'

'Er... no.'

'So what are you doing here?'

'I left something behind in my locker,' said Hayley. 'I just popped in to pick it up. Who are you working with today?'

'Joan Cross.'

'I don't want to bump into her. She gave me a real telling-off yesterday for being so distracted. Is she still in the staffroom?'

'She'll have gone to set up the machine by now.'

'I'll slip straight in and out, then.'

'By the way, what did you forget, Hayley?'

'Oh, just a few magazines. See you, Suzie.'

Hayley left and Suzie got the list of patients from the receptionist. She asked the first three to step into the cubicles and change into their gowns. Suzie was just about to leave reception, when she saw someone peering in through the swing door. When he caught her eye, he retreated quickly and let the door close.

The man was Dennis Reynolds, who'd had a chest X-ray earlier in the week. Suzie wondered why he'd come back. She also remembered that his set of X-rays was one of the sets that had gone missing for a short time from the storage unit. Why had Hayley and Dennis Reynolds both turned up unexpectedly?

———/\/———

Bella had realized how selfish she was being. After hours of thinking about it, she decided she owed Carl an apology. Instead of putting herself first all the time, she ought to be considering him. She would never keep his friendship if she tried to hold him back.

They'd arranged to meet in a café that morning and she was there first. When he came in, Carl seemed rather flustered as he sat down beside her.

'I can't stay long, I'm afraid, Suzie. Something's come up. It's an appointment I was hoping to get out of, Bella. But I can't, unfortunately. So I'll have to leave in half-an-hour.'

'Is that all I'm going to see of you?'

'I can probably see you later on this evening.'

'But you promised me lunch!'

'That was before this other thing came up.'

Bella was about to complain when she remembered the decision she'd just reached. She shouldn't hassle Carl. His work came first and she had to fit in with it. If they only had thirty minutes together, she didn't want to waste them by arguing with him. Bella gave him a big smile.

'Sorry, Carl,' she said. 'I was silly last night. If you have a chance of a research post at St Catherine's, I ought to be jumping for joy. It's an honour. Instead of that, all I could think about was myself. It was horrible of me.'

'No, it wasn't. It just showed you cared.'

'I do, Carl – about you and your career. Take the post at St Catherine's.'

'You're doing it again!' he said, laughing. 'Getting me jobs that I haven't even been interviewed for yet. There'll be a lot of competition, Bella. They may well choose someone else at St Catherine's.'

'Not if they've got any sense.'

The waitress came up and they ordered coffee and croissants. Bella studied him carefully. Carl was wearing his suit again and she found that reassuring somehow.

'Who interviewed you at City Hospital?' she asked.

'Three of their management team, and the Personnel Officer was there, as well.'

'Damian said they usually have a medical man on the interview panel. Doctors are the best judges of doctors. When Damian was interviewed, they had a consultant on the team.'

'So did we, Bella. Let me see if I can remember his name,' he said, thinking hard. 'Got it! It was Gilbert Buchanan.'

'Oh, he's the best we've got!'

'Yes, he was really tough.'

'If you got Gilbert Buchanan's approval, you must be good. He's famous. He's always getting his name in the papers. I said you'd be a second Gilbert Buchanan!'

'I'd rather be a first Carl Mullen!'

They laughed. Bella felt so much better now that she'd overcome her own selfish feelings. She knew she had to trust Carl and her friendship with him. She wouldn't make the mistake of doubting him again. Unlike most of her other boyfriends, he wasn't just a young guy in search of a good time. Carl was a serious person, who was only interested in a relationship that had meaning.

'When are you going to come to our house?' she asked. 'I want you to meet my friends.'

'I will, Bella. Soon.'

'Don't you want to see where I live?'

'I've dropped you off,' said Carl.

'All you saw was the outside. Why not come in next time?'

'Because I prefer to be alone with you.'

'Come tomorrow night then. They'll all be out for hours. We'd have the house to ourselves then.'

'Are you sure?'

'Quite sure. It's lovely to sit in a car with you, but my room is a lot nicer. Wouldn't you like to?'

Carl thought it over. He grinned at her.

'All right, I'll come. Tomorrow night.'

'Great!'

'Find out when your friends are going out and then it'll be your turn to interview me.'

'I don't need to,' said Bella, smiling. 'I'll give you the job without a second thought. I'm all yours!'

Gordy was holding his arms straight up in the air.

'How much longer are you going to be?' he asked.

'Just keep still, Gordy.'

'But my arms are aching!'

'I'm having trouble with this belt.'

'Hurry up, Marco. I feel as if I'm in a bank

while it's being robbed. Hands up or we shoot! It hurts!'

'There!' said Mark, finally securing the belt. 'You can put your arms down now.'

'Thank goodness.'

Gordy was about to go to *The White Horse* pub again and he'd enlisted Mark's help. With the belt in place around his chest, the small tape recorder could now be attached to it with thick tape. When that was done, Mark plugged in the microphone.

'Where should this go?'

'Somewhere out of sight.'

'Your shirt pocket?'

'Use my handkerchief,' said Gordy, taking it out of his pocket. 'It'll conceal the microphone and help to hold it in position.'

Mark did as he was told, then stood back to admire the result.

'Put your jacket on, Gordy.'

'OK.' He slipped it on. 'How's that?'

'Terrible! The tape recorder's showing and there's a lump in your coat where the microphone is pressing up against it. You'll have to wear something bigger. Like a puffa jacket.'

'It's too warm for that.'

'Sweat it out. It's all in a good cause.'

Gordy found his puffa and put it on. It hung much more loosely and covered up the tape

145

recorder and the microphone.

'It's too thick, Marco. It'll muffle the sound. Stand by.' He switched on the machine. 'Say something.'

'Nurses are underpaid. Double their wages at once.'

'That's enough,' said Gordy, stopping the tape and running it back. 'Here we go.'

Mark's voice could be heard clearly and Gordy was satisfied.

'OK, I'm off, Marco.'

'Let me come with you.'

'No. This is my fight. Besides, I'd hate to come between a man and his telly. I know you love Saturday evenings!'

'*Casualty* is on!'

'Then I'm glad I'm going out. It'll remind me of the day they carried me into Casualty after that demo.'

'Be careful, Gordy.'

'You sound like Kirsty.'

'How is she, by the way?'

'I never get close enough to find out. That dog of hers, Dodo – every time Kirsty and I try to have a moment together, we've got a Dalmation jumping all over us!'

Mark laughed. 'You're in favour of Animal Welfare, aren't you?' he said.

'Not in Dodo's case – she's a menace.'

Gordy checked his face in the mirror and gave Mark a farewell grin.

'If I'm not back by midnight, send in the SAS.'

Mark went back into the living room to switch on the television. He liked being alone in the house on a Saturday evening – lots of his favourite programmes were on then. As he dropped on to the sofa, he saw that he was just in time to catch the end of the local news. A sports correspondent reported that the striker for the City football team had broken his leg in a cup match that afternoon. Film of the incident came up on the screen.

Running towards the penalty area with the ball, the striker tried to go past the full back, and was tripped up, mercilessly. He rolled on the ground in agony. The crowd erupted! The team's physiotherapist came racing on, but he saw at once that the leg was broken and signalled for a stretcher. While the referee booked the full back, the injured man was carried off on a stretcher by four St John Ambulance Men.

Mark sat forward suddenly. His interest was aroused by something else. He looked different in uniform, but Mark felt certain that it was him – Carl was part of the St John Ambulance team!0

Gordy didn't have long to wait at the pub. Jacko and Phil came in with another man. They elbowed their way to the bar and bought themselves pints of beer. Since all the seats were taken, they found a place to stand in the corner. The noise was an unforeseen hazard. Gordy hadn't realized that *The White Horse* would be so full. He had grave doubts about his microphone being able to pick up much of what the youths were saying.

He decided to wait until some of the customers left. When the hubbub had calmed down slightly, he gave up his seat and bought himself another drink. Then he edged his way over to the corner where the three youths were still talking.

Jacko was clearly their leader. He was bigger than the others and much more forceful. He had a round face, a broken nose and very short hair. Phil had a solid build and he was shorter and darker. The third guy was a skinny teenager, with a mad giggle. He nodded as Jacko did the talking.

'I think we should go for it, lads.'

'It's too soon, Jacko,' argued Phil.

'We've got to hit them again.'

'But it's a morning demo. I'd have a job getting

the time off. Maybe this is one to miss.'

'I'm not going to miss it,' said Jacko. 'My gaffer will be only too glad to give me a morning off when I tell him what it's for. Anyway, it's only a small demo. A dozen of us could break it up – no trouble.'

'Yes, Jacko!' said the skinny youth, grinning.

'You up for it, Neil?'

'Count me in.'

'Good. Phil?'

'I'll try, Jacko. You know I hate to miss out on the action.'

Gordy was close enough to overhear most of this and he switched on his tape recorder. With luck, he might have picked up the drift of their conversation. It suddenly stopped. When Gordy turned to see why, he found himself staring straight into Jacko's angry eyes.

'What are you doing?' demanded the thug.

'Nothing,' said Gordy, shrugging.

'You was listening to us, wasn't you?'

'Haven't we seen you somewhere before?' said Phil.

'No, not me.' Gordy shook his head frantically.

'Who are you?' said Jacko, with a menacing scowl.

'I just came in for a drink, that's all.'

'Pull the other one, mate.'

Gordy made a sudden switch of plan. Since they'd caught him eavesdropping, he tried to turn it to his advantage. He tried to make his voice sound much rougher.

'All right,' he said. 'I didn't come in by accident. I wanted to meet you. The barman told me you come in now and then. Your name's Jacko, isn't it?'

'Yeah, so what?'

'And he's Phil.'

'How do you know that?' said Phil.

'The barman told me. I was drinking in here the other day, talking to him about that protest march. The one that turned into a riot. I saw it on the telly.'

Jacko glared at him. 'So?' he challenged.

'I just wished I'd been part of it, that's all.'

'What? The demo?'

'No,' said Gordy. 'The gang who broke it up. They knew what they were doing. It was well organized.'

'That was Jacko's doing,' said the skinny youth.

'Shut up, Neil!'

'Sorry, Jacko.'

'I hate these do-gooders,' sneered Gordy. 'They're always marching around with banners.

Stop this, free that, save whales, give elephants the vote. It gets on my nerves!' Gordy was really getting into the part.

'And ours,' said Phil.

'It's about time somebody struck back at them.'

'And is that what you'd like to do?' said Jacko.

'You bet!'

'What's your name?'

'Roy – I'm an unemployed brickie.'

'So you're free during the day then, are you?'

'Yeah, that's right.'

Jacko stepped aside and had a brief conference with Phil. They sized Gordy up then decided that his interest was genuine.

'OK,' said Jacko, 'you're in.'

'Great! What's it to be, then? Another pint for everyone?'

Jacko grinned. 'You're definitely in, mate!'

Gordy was making more progress than he'd expected.

Karlene went off to the hospital early on Sunday morning, but not to work in Physiotherapy. She wanted a dip in the swimming pool. Working with patients in the pool had revived her own interest in swimming and now she could manage thirty lengths quite easily.

She changed into her bikini and jumped into the pool. Soon, splashing told her that she wasn't the only one there. Zack was swimming down the pool with a leisurely breaststroke. What surprised Karlene was that he was wearing a black T-shirt as well as his swimming trunks.

'Hi, Zack!' she called.

Her voice echoed around the swimming pool and startled him. He swam to the side of the pool and held the bar.

'I didn't know you'd be here, Karlene.'

'I felt like a dip to wake me up.'

'Me, too.'

'How long have you been here?'

'Over an hour.'

'But you live miles away from here,' she said. 'You must have got up at the crack of dawn!'

'I was up, anyway. I haven't been sleeping too well.'

'Neither has she.'

'Who?'

'Hayley.'

Zack nodded, sadly. He clearly had many regrets about his break-up with Hayley but he wasn't ready to talk about them. Karlene didn't want to press him.

'Look out!' she said, as she dived in at the deep

end and swam a length just to get the feel of the water. She made her way across to Zack and held on to the bar. She noticed that he kept his body under the water.

'Have you spoken to her lately?' he asked. 'How is she?'

'Pretty miserable.'

'That makes two of us.'

'Hayley still isn't sure what happened between you two.'

'Neither am I,' he admitted.

'In that case, you're better off apart,' said Karlene. 'Not that I'm offering any advice here,' she added, quickly. 'I'm no agony aunt. I'm keeping out of it from now on.'

'You got caught in the middle, that's all. I lost out,' he said, wistfully. 'I know that now.'

'Hayley feels the same.'

Zack nodded and pushed off from the edge, lying on his back and using only his feet to propel him through the surface of the water. Karlene watched him for a few moments then swam across to him.

'This is not her fault at all, is it, Zack?' she said. 'Hayley hasn't done anything wrong.'

'Not really.'

'So why does she have to suffer?'

'Because she was bothering me too much,

Karlene. Crowding me. I need some breathing space.'

'You didn't always give *Hayley* any breathing space. You were round at her flat every five minutes.'

'Well... yes,' Zack admitted.

'Doesn't that give her certain rights?'

'I suppose so.'

'You can't just dump her without an explanation.'

'I told you – we had that big row.'

'Why don't you tell Hayley why it happened then?'

'I thought you weren't going to give me any more advice?' he said, sharply. 'I knew you'd gang up against me. I just want to be left alone, Karlene.'

He swam fast to the side of the pool and got out. When she saw his T-shirt, Karlene suddenly realized what Zack's problem might be. It was worth a try, anyway.

'You can't go on lying to yourself forever, Zack. That's why you won't let her near you, isn't it?' Karlene swam across to the edge of the pool and looked up at him.

'You think there's something wrong with you, don't you?' said Karlene. 'And you won't face up to it. When are you going to go to the doctor?'

Zack looked hurt. All his strength seemed to flow out of him. He shook his head and shrugged, helplessly.

'I'm frightened, Karlene.'

———⋀———

Bella couldn't get rid of him. What made it worse was that Mark insisted on talking to her about Carl.

'It was him, Bella,' he said. 'I know it was.'

'Don't be silly!'

'Carl was helping to carry that stretcher.'

'He's a qualified doctor, not a member of the St John Ambulance Brigade. They're all part-time amateurs.'

'I still think it was him.'

'You hardly know Carl. You've only seen him once.' Bella refused to listen to any more. She bustled him out and Mark went off to meet some friends for a drink. Everybody else was out, so the house was empty. Bella waited five minutes, then stepped out on to the pavement to give her pre-arranged signal. Carl was waiting in his Metro at the end of the road. He drove up and parked near the house.

Bella brought him straight into the living room. 'I thought Mark would never leave,' she said.

'What was the problem?'

'He had this crazy idea that he saw you on telly last night. In the sports news!'

'Oh?' said Carl, in a neutral voice.

'Some guy broke his leg in a football match, and the St John's Ambulance Team carried him off. Mark claims you were one of them.'

'Your friend's got very good eyesight.'

'What do you mean, Carl?'

'It must have been Liam, my brother. He was on duty at a soccer match yesterday.'

'I thought Liam was an art student.'

'He is, Bella. But he belongs to the St John's Ambulance in his spare time. Rather sad, really. We come from a medical family, remember. Liam didn't have the academic qualifications to become a doctor, so he took up art instead. Being in the St John Ambulance means he can at least get to play at being a doctor.'

'So Mark *was* right.'

'Up to a point. Liam looks quite like me.'

Bella gazed at him, smiling. He grinned back at her and pulled her into his arms. He started to kiss her but she drew back slightly.

'Are you having more doubts about me, Bella?'

'No, of course not.'

'I'm a doctor, Bella. I've proved that to you.'

'Yes,' she said. 'A real doctor and a real man!'

'So what are we waiting for?'

Bella's hesitation vanished. She hugged him tight. She'd been thinking about this moment all day and she didn't want to waste one precious moment of it. Carl was hers at last!

Without letting go of each other, they moved to the sofa and sank down on to it. Carl kissed her and she pulled him even closer. They were soon lying entwined on the sofa.

Neither of them even heard the telephone at first. It was Bella who finally registered that it was ringing and ringing.

'I'd better answer it, in case it's important.'

'Be quick, Bella!'

'I will.' She picked up the receiver. 'Hello?'

'Bella, is that you! It's Jasmine here,' she gasped.

'Jasmine, are you OK?"

'Yes, but Bella, the baby's on its way!'

'Are you sure?'

'Yes,' breathed Jasmine. 'The waters broke. And now I've gone into labour. What should I do?'

'Call an ambulance. They'll bring you straight to the hospital.'

'What's up?' asked Carl, moving across to Bella.

She turned to him. 'That friend I told you

about? Jasmine? She's gone into labour and she's frightened out of her wits.'

'Are you still there, Bella?' cried Jasmine. 'I'm on my own. I'm scared!'

'Dial 999, Jasmine.'

'We can get there faster than the ambulance,' said Carl, firmly. 'Tell her we're on our way!'

'What about our evening together?'

'Your friend's in distress. This is an emergency.'

'You're right,' decided Bella. She spoke into the telephone again. 'Jasmine?'

'Yes.'

'Ring for an ambulance and sit tight. We're on our way!'

Gordy didn't like police stations. It was the second time in twenty-four hours that he'd been to this one, and he did so with some reluctance. Kirsty went with him but Dodo had been left behind. Gordy felt he'd exchanged a policeman with four legs and a tail for the real thing!

'Yes?' said the desk sergeant. 'Can I help you?'

'I came in last night,' explained Gordy. 'I spoke to Detective-Sergeant Roberts, about that riot earlier in the week, and I left a tape recording with him.'

'One moment, sir.'

The sergeant made a phone call and nodded as he was given instructions from a voice at the other end of the line. When he put the receiver down, he pointed to a door.

'Step into that interview room, please, sir,' he said. 'DS Roberts will be with you directly.'

'Thanks, officer.'

Gordy and Kirsty went into a bleak room with bare walls. It contained three plastic chairs and a formica table. They both shivered involuntarily.

'Makes you feel like a suspect, doesn't it?' said Gordy.

'I am one.'

'They've got nothing on you, Kirst.'

'Then why did they lock me up here?'

'They were too heavy-handed, they over-reacted. Let's hope they catch the real troublemakers now.'

Detective-Sergeant Roberts came into the room. He was a wiry man in his thirties with a neat moustache. He invited them to sit down then took the seat opposite them.

'Thank you for coming back, Mr Robbins,' he said.

'Have you had a chance to listen to the tape yet?'

'Yes. It's not very clear, I'm afraid, but we were able to pick up enough of what they were saying.'

'So you heard Jacko and Phil?'

'More or less.'

'And you know they started that riot?'

'It looks that way, Sir, yes.'

'Are you going to arrest them, then?'

'Hold on a minute, Sir.'

'They're on that video recording, too. Attacking us.'

'The trouble is we don't know their real names or where they live,' said the detective. 'The only place we might find them is *The White Horse* pub and my lads are not too popular down there. If I send a plain clothes man into that pub, these two characters won't go near the place.'

'You've got to catch them!' urged Kirsty.

'We will, miss. All in good time, when they try to break up the next protest march. Thanks to your friend here, we know when and where the attack will be. That's the time to get these two – when we can catch them in the act, and collar their mates, as well.' He turned to Gordy. 'We need your co-operation here, Mr Robbins.'

'What do I have to do?'

'Go along with everything they say.'

'Join the attack, you mean?'

'Yes,' said the detective. 'If you disappear, they'll smell a rat and call off their sabotage. You must make them think you're one of them.'

'That's too dangerous!' said Kirsty.

'He's managed pretty well so far, miss.'

'Yes,' said Gordy. 'I quite enjoyed it.'

'We'll make a copper out of you yet, Sir.'

'You could get hurt, Gordy,' warned Kirsty.

'Nothing can be worse than last time. Besides, I won't actually attack the demonstrators myself. As soon as the aggro starts, I'll get out!'

'We'll have teams of men hidden on all sides.'

'A police ambush?'

'Yes, Sir. We'll beat them at their own game.'

As the detective outlined his plan, Gordy

began to feel more relaxed. His help had been valuable, after all. He'd given the police the evidence they needed to pursue the real thugs behind the riot. Jacko and Phil might soon be sitting in the very chairs that Gordy and Kirsty were occupying now.

Kirsty was tense and nervous. The strain of being there was telling on her. She was still under threat of prosecution herself and she felt very uncomfortable.

'Have you studied that video recording?' asked Gordy.

'Very carefully, Sir, yes,' said Roberts.

'Then you know that we were set on by that gang?'

'No doubt about that.'

'Did you see that guy, Jacko, hit me with the pole?'

'Yes, sir. And he enjoyed every minute of it.'

'That's more than I did,' said Gordy, rubbing the back of his head. 'What about the charges against Kirsty?

'What charges?'

'Damage to property and striking a policewoman, I believe.'

'Now we've studied the video, we take a very different view. The damage was accidental and there was clearly no intention on Miss Longdon's part to strike my colleague, WPC Ridley.'

'I didn't even know she was there,' said Kirsty.

'That was obvious. You hit out in self-defence.'

'I'm glad you understand that now.'

'We do, Miss.'

'So what happens to Kirst now?' asked Gordy.

'The charges have been dropped.'

'Thank heavens!' said Kirsty, throwing herself into Gordy's arms with relief. 'It's such a load off my mind!'

'What did I tell you, Kirst?'

'Thank you, Gordy!' She gave him a big kiss.

Roberts smiled and tapped the table. 'Now, now, you two,' he said. 'None of that here. I think you should take the young lady off somewhere to celebrate.'

'You bet!' said Gordy.

———/\/———

Carl drove at a reckless speed through the streets. Bella was guiding him and she was grateful when the double-decker bus finally came into sight. The car screeched to a halt and Bella jumped out and dashed into the bus. Carl grabbed his doctor's bag and followed her. Jasmine's groans were coming from upstairs.

'It's all right, Jasmine,' said Bella, running up, 'we're here.'

'Thank goodness!' said Jasmine.

She was lying on the bed, covered in perspiration. Bella introduced Carl and he knelt down to examine Jasmine. Both of them felt reassured by his presence.

'Did you ring for an ambulance?' asked Bella.

'No,' said Jasmine. 'I was in such a panic that I dropped the phone. It's under the mattress somewhere. I just didn't have the strength to look for it.'

Bella was horrified. 'No ambulance on its way?'

'We can manage here,' said Carl, confidently.

'But what if anything goes wrong?' asked Bella, as she searched frantically on the floor for the mobile phone. 'They've got all the facilities at the hospital. That's where Jasmine should be.'

She found the phone and switched it on. There was no tone. She tried again – but she still couldn't get a line.

'It's not working!' she said, desperately.

'It's my fault,' gasped Jasmine. 'It just flew out of my hand. I'll pay to have it repaired, I promise.'

'Don't worry about that now, Jasmine. You need an ambulance. Where's the nearest phone box?'

'Just at the end of the road, Bella.'

'And where's everyone else?'

'They've gone to the pub. You'll pass it on the way.'

'I'll dig them out. They should be here with you.'

'It was my idea,' sighed Jasmine. 'I felt so sleepy that I didn't want to go out, but I didn't want to stop their fun. I told them to go. If I'd known the number of the pub, I'd have rung for Raphael to come back – or Baz.'

'I'll get both of them!' vowed Bella. 'Can you manage here on your own, Carl?'

'Yes,' he said, putting the ends of the stethoscope into his ears. 'Everything's under control. Just relax, Jasmine. You're in good hands. Now, start breathing deeply.'

Bella was reassured. A doctor was coping and now the priority was to get an ambulance. She raced down the stairs and sprinted the length of the road to the phone box. Dialling the emergency number, she asked to be put through to the hospital.

'There's someone here having a baby!' she said, gasping for breath. 'We need an ambulance as soon as possible.'

After giving directions, she came out of the phone box and ran back to the pub. *The Jolly Sailor* had several rowdy customers in. She could hear the noise as she approached, but it was no time for niceties. Bella charged straight into the lounge bar.

'Jasmine's baby is coming!' she yelled. 'She needs the father. Where is he?'

Both Baz and Raphael came hurtling through the door.

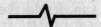

Gordy poured two glasses of wine to celebrate and handed one to Kirsty. They clinked their glasses and sipped the wine, sitting together on the sofa. Gordy had brought Kirsty back to the house and found it deserted. No friends and – most important of all – no Dodo! There was nothing to stop him now. He let Kirsty's admiration wash over him.

'I can't tell you how relieved I am, Gordy.'

'You've been through a grim time, Kirst.'

'And it's all over now - thanks to you!'

'I was determined to catch them, Kirsty.'

'You took such a risk.'

'Yes,' he said, airily. 'There was a point in the pub when I thought they'd sussed me but I managed to talk my way out of it. I always fancied myself as a detective, to be honest. Maybe the police will use me again.'

Kirsty smiled. 'No,' she said. 'I don't think so, Gordy.'

He slipped an arm around her and drank some more wine.

'What a perfect way to spend a Sunday evening.'

'Yes,' she agreed. 'Anything on the telly?'

'The telly! When you've got me as entertainment?'

She giggled. 'I was only teasing.'

Kirsty was her old self again. With the fear of prosecution lifted, she could start to enjoy herself once more. Gordy kissed her hand. She put her glass aside and before he knew it, Gordy was flat out on the sofa with Kirsty on top of him. He couldn't believe his luck!

'I just want to thank you, Gordy,' she murmured. 'You saved me yet again.'

She kissed him passionately and didn't even notice when they fell to the floor. The sound of the front door made them leap apart. Mark came in, looking surprised.

'Oh!' he said, looking down at them. 'Sorry to barge in at an awkward moment.'

'That's all right, Mark,' said Kirsty, giggling.

'It isn't all right,' snapped Gordy. 'Buzz off, Mark.'

'I came back to see Bella. It's important.'

'She's not here,' said Gordy, getting up. 'There's a note by the telephone.'

Mark snatched it up and read it hurriedly. 'Oh no! This is terrible!'

'What is?' asked Kirsty.

'Jasmine's baby is on its way and Bella has raced over there with Doctor Carl Mullen.'

'Nothing wrong with that,' said Gordy.

'There is,' said Mark, grimly. 'Carl isn't a doctor at all. I've just had a drink with Damian. There were no interviews at the hospital last week! It's all a lie. Carl Mullen is a complete fraud. He's been stringing Bella along!'

'But why?' asked Kirsty.

'To impress her, of course.'

'But didn't he help that boy who got knocked down?'

'Yes,' said Mark. 'He can do that. He belongs to the St John Ambulance. But he's no more a qualified doctor than I am!'

'Just a minute,' said Gordy. 'Didn't you say he'd gone over to this friend of yours – Jasmine, isn't it?'

'Yes. The baby's on its way.'

'What does Carl think he's going to do?'

'Deliver it, I expect,' said Mark, looking horrified.

'But he's not qualified!'

'Jasmine doesn't know that. Neither does Bella.'

'This is awful,' said Gordy, realizing the implications. 'If there are complications with the birth, he won't have a clue what to do. We must get there, fast!'

'And I know how!' Mark snatched up the telephone. 'I lent Jasmine that mobile phone of Suzie's. The number's written down here somewhere.' He found it on the pad and dialled frantically. 'Continuous tone – it's switched off.'

Kirsty gasped. 'You can't leave that poor girl in the hands of a fake doctor. Do something, Gordy!'

'Drive me over there,' decided Mark.

'Do you know the way?'

'I think so. Just pray that we're in time.'

'Posing as a doctor is a serious offence,' said Gordy. 'The police will be after him for this.'

'Baz and Raphael will beat them to it, I should think. They're the joint fathers,' said Mark. 'If Carl Mullen does anything to harm Jasmine or the baby, they'll tear him to pieces. Come on! There's no time to waste!'

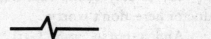

Jasmine was in real distress. As she felt another contraction, she twisted about on the mattress, groaning. With his coat off, Carl sat beside her, trying to soothe her, taking her through her breathing exercises and assuring her that all would be well. Bella watched with alarm. Even though she worked in the Maternity Hospital, she'd never actually been present at a birth, and wasn't sure if Jasmine's symptoms were normal.

The three other girls who shared the bus with Jasmine were downstairs, boiling water on their gas stove in case it was needed. Baz and Raphael were pacing up and down outside the bus, waiting for the ambulance.

'It's moving!' said Jasmine. 'I can feel it!'

'Just relax, Jasmine. Take it easy,' urged Carl.

'Nobody told me it would be like this.'

'Try to stay calm,' said Bella. 'You've got a doctor here, don't worry.'

'And a nurse,' said Carl. 'We can manage between us.'

'We can't deliver the baby!' said Bella, alarmed.

'We may have to, Bella.'

'Have you ever done this before?' she asked,

panic rising in her voice.

'Of course,' he said. 'I did a year in Obstetrics.'

'Ah!' moaned Jasmine, as another contraction came.

Ellie came upstairs with a large kettle of hot water and an enamel bowl. Over her arm were some clean towels.

'Put them there, please,' said Carl.

'OK, doctor,' said Ellie, putting everything beside the mattress. 'How are you feeling, Jas?'

'The pain's eased off a little.'

'Raphael sends his love. And Baz.'

Ellie went back downstairs. If the top of the bus was going to be turned into a delivery ward, there was no room in there for her.

Carl rolled up his sleeves and washed his hands in the bowl, before drying them on the towel. Then he took some talcum powder from his bag and shook it on to his hands. When it was rubbed in, he slipped on a pair of medical gloves, taken from a sealed packet.

'You'd better wash your hands as well, Bella.'

'The ambulance should be here any minute.' Bella was getting frantic.

'Just in case, OK?'

'Ahhhhh!' Jasmine let out a deep cry as a series of contractions came. She felt as if the baby was about to be born. Jasmine's moans went on and on and Bella was worried, turning to Carl for advice.

But quite suddenly he started to lose his nerve. Grabbing his bag, he took out a textbook and thumbed through the pages, madly.

'Carl, what are you *doing?*' she asked, alarmed.

'Just a minute, Bella.'

'Jasmine's in pain. Please help her, tell her what to do!'

'Be quiet!' he snapped.

Realization hit Bella with the force of a blow! Carl Mullen didn't know what to do. Now that he was confronted with a real emergency, he couldn't cope. Helping a boy who was knocked off his bike was one thing – he could do that very well. But delivering a baby was beyond him!

Bella felt sick. She'd put Jasmine's baby into the hands of someone who wasn't competent to deliver it. Carl Mullen was no longer calm and authoritative. His face was ashen and his eyes began to look desperate, as he flicked through the pages of his medical textbook.

Luckily, Jasmine was so caught up in her own pain and anxiety that she didn't notice what Carl was doing. She still had naive faith in him. Why should she doubt him? As she emitted another series of groans, Carl almost dropped his book. He turned back to her and began to wipe her brow with a towel dipped in cold water.

Bella looked at him with a mixture of anger and disgust. It was one thing to let her down – she'd been far too trusting and deserved it. But Jasmine was something else. She was in extreme distress and needed proper professional help – and that was clearly beyond him.

'I'm not sure what will happen next,' he admitted, in a complete panic now.

'Don't touch her!' said Bella.

In the distance, they heard the wail of the ambulance, approaching at speed. Bella sighed with relief. Jasmine and the baby were saved.

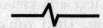

Karlene met her at the hospital. It was half-way between their two houses and they'd gone to a nearby cafe. Hayley had put on her best dress in an effort to cheer herself up, but her sadness was too deep to dispel. They found a table and brought over their coffee.

'How's it going?' asked Karlene.

'It isn't.'

'You still miss him a lot, don't you?'

'Like anything, Karlene. Though I'd never admit that to Zack. He treated me badly and I won't forget that in a hurry.'

'You might, Hayley. In time.'

'What do you mean?'

173

'I met him in the swimming pool this morning.'

'Zack?'

'He was wearing a black T-shirt in the pool and I suddenly realized he might be trying to hide something – from himself as much as from anyone else.'

'I don't understand, Karlene.'

'Why do you think he wouldn't let you get close to him?'

'Because he went off me, of course.'

'No, Hayley. He was afraid that one thing would lead to another and you'd both finish up with no clothes on. Then you'd see what was wrong with his shoulder.'

'His *shoulder*?

'This is in the strictest confidence, Hayley.'

'Yes, yes. Just tell me. You're scaring the life out of me.'

'It took me ages to get it out of him.'

'What's wrong with Zack's shoulder?'

'He's got this lump on it. Some sort of growth.'

'Oh, no!' gasped Hayley. 'Why didn't he say?'

'Because he was too embarrassed about it. And he hasn't been to the doctor because he's afraid to find out the truth.' Karlene gave a wry smile. 'Stupid, isn't it? He works in a hospital but he won't take advantage of the facilities. That lump

174

sent him into a complete panic.'

'Why? What does he think it is?'

'He imagines the worst. A malignant tumour.'

'Did he let you see it?'

'No, Hayley,' said Karlene, 'but he did listen to my advice. He's going to the doctor first thing in the morning. Whatever the problem is, it's time to face up to it.'

'Poor Zack! He must have been going through hell.'

'Hurting you gave him the biggest pain,' she said.

'I must go to him now.'

'No, Hayley,' insisted her friend. 'Wait until he's seen the doctor. My guess is he'll come looking for you, then.'

Hayley took time to absorb what she'd just heard. It explained Zack's strange behaviour and his reluctance to let her near him. But she was hurt that he hadn't confided in her, so that she could offer moral support. But at least there was one consolation: Zack still liked her.

———⋀———

Suzie had only meant to pop in to the X-ray Department for a moment. She'd forgotten to take her uniform home to wash it. If she left it to dry overnight, it would be ready to bring back to the hospital on Monday morning. The X-ray Department was closed, so she was surprised to see a light under the door of the storage unit. It was supposed to be kept locked all day on Sunday.

Her suspicions were immediately aroused. She felt certain that Hayley was in there. The mystery of the missing X-rays might be solved at last. Creeping up to the door, she took hold of the handle and yanked it open.

'What are *you* doing in here?' asked Suzie.

But she wasn't looking at Hayley. The person who was putting stickers on some of the X-rays, was Joan Cross. When she saw she'd been caught, the radiographer burst into tears.

———⌇———

Gordy was driving too fast. He kept missing turns and Mark got increasingly confused. They kept having to double back, as Mark tried to remember the way he and Bella had first come. The sound of the ambulance gave them all the guidance they needed. Gordy followed it and turned into the right road at last. The ambulance was parked outside the double-decker bus, and the paramedics were running in with a stretcher. Baz and Raphael were waiting anxiously outside.

Gordy accelerated, bringing his car to a skidding halt. They were just in time to see Carl

Mullen coming out of the bus with Bella at his heels. She was seething with fury. Mark, Gordy and Kirsty got out of the car in time to hear what Bella was saying.

'That was criminal!' she yelled at Carl. 'You let her believe that you were a real doctor, and Jasmine trusted you!'

'I *am* a real doctor. You saw my certificate.'

'I saw you go into a panic!'

'Everything would have been all right.'

'You didn't have a clue what to do, Carl!'

'No, he didn't,' said Mark, coming up to them. 'He's been lying to you, Bella. He's a fraud. He didn't have an interview at the hospital at all.'

'I did,' argued Carl, looking flustered. 'Gilbert Buchanan was there!'

'He couldn't have been,' said Kirsty. 'I'm his secretary and I know what all his appointments are. He wasn't involved in interviews last week.'

'Then it must have been another consultant.'

'Give up,' said Gordy, bluntly. 'We know the truth.'

A groan from Jasmine made them all turn round. She was being carried out on a stretcher and put into the ambulance. Baz and Raphael went with her, as it sped off towards the hospital. Bella was relieved that her friend was in good hands at last. Now she could really get angry!

'You're a two-faced, lying hypocrite!' she yelled.

'Calm down, Bella,' said Carl.

'You're a complete *crook*.'

'They'll lock you up for this,' warned Mark.

'Yes,' said Gordy, grabbing him. 'Who *are* you, any way?'

Carl saw his game was up. Escape was the only answer. Swinging his doctor's bag, he hit Gordy in the stomach, making him double up with pain. Then he hurled the bag in Mark's face. By the time the two of them recovered, Carl had jumped into his car and driven off.

Gordy and Mark ran to the Astra and jumped in. They were soon chasing Carl at top speed.

'Get him, Gordy!' shouted Kirsty, after them.

'Take him to the police!' yelled Bella.

But it was all too much for her. When Bella remembered how much effort and love she'd put into her friendship with Carl, she was devastated. She'd trusted him completely and all he was was a bogus doctor. It made her feel such a failure! She turned away so that Kirsty couldn't see her tears.

Meanwhile, Gordy was driving like someone possessed. He swung round corners, skidded round bends and even shot through red lights. He was determined to keep the Metro in sight. Carl was taking dangerous risks, too, as his car mounted the pavement and then bounced back on to the road at a dizzy speed.

Strapped in his safety belt, Mark was still trying to work out why Carl had done such a thing.

'Why did he do it, Gordy?' he said.

'There are lots of fake doctors, Mark.'

'But most of them are after money – not Carl.'

'He's a fraud. That's all that matters, Mark.'

'It isn't. There has to be a reason.'

Gordy ignored him, jamming his foot down even harder on the accelerator. They were in the High Street now, curling past the point where Gordy had been attacked during the march. As the road straightened out ahead, they could see the hospital in the distance. Gordy chose his moment.

Shooting along at top speed, he gradually gained on the Metro until he was able to draw level. They powered on, side-by-side, until the road narrowed ahead to one lane. There wasn't room for both cars and Gordy was determined not to give way, coaxing a last burst of speed out of his engine. Carl tried to do the same, but then lost his nerve completely.

Jamming on the brakes, he went into a skid, the driving wheel knocked from his hands. The car spun like a Catherine Wheel towards the middle of the road. It demolished two bollards before it came to a halt against a concrete lamp post. Carl was dazed but unhurt. Gordy stopped his car and ran back down the road, with Mark at his heels. They were relieved that there was no blood visible.

Gordy opened the door and helped Carl out.

'I'll ask you again,' said Gordy. 'Who *are* you?'

'My name is Liam Mullen,' he spluttered.

'Oh yes, so what happened to Doctor Carl Mullen?'

'He's my brother. He's a GP in Dublin.'

With that, he passed out in Gordy's arms. Mark smiled grimly, pointing across to the hospital on the other side of the road.

'He had a doctor's instinct, anyway,' said Mark. 'He crashed right outside Casualty. Let's get him over there, fast.'

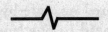

Karlene was making the meal that evening, and the aroma of lasagne was drifting out of the oven. Suzie set the plates on the table.

'How many of us are eating in?' she asked.

'Four,' said Karlene. 'Gordy's going out for a big celebration with Kirsty. He deserves it.'

'Yes. That information he gave the police made all the difference. When those thugs tried to disrupt another protest march, they were caught red-handed. The police were delighted with the help they got from Gordy. He's a real hero!'

'They said I'd make a good detective,' said Gordy, as he walked in on their conversation. 'A plain clothes man.'

Suzie and Karlene burst out laughing. He was wearing his bright green jacket, his check trousers and his striped shirt. His polka-dot tie could be seen a hundred metres away.

'Go on,' said Gordy, 'laugh away. Thanks to me, the boys in blue nabbed Jacko and Phil. They were the ringleaders.'

'Why did they do it?' asked Karlene.

'Those yobs just like a fight,' said Suzie.

'There was more to it than that,' explained

Gordy. 'Phil is a butcher. Jacko worked in the meat market. Butchers have suffered a lot over the past few years. Less meat is being sold and the Animal Welfare lobby and the Veggie crowd have made a lot of noise. Jacko and Phil decided to strike back. We were unlucky enough to be the target.'

'The rest of that mob weren't butchers,' said Suzie.

'They were just there for the action.'

'Not any more.'

'No,' said Gordy, sticking out his chest. 'With my help, the police were able to round up the whole gang.'

'You're not the only detective around here,' said Karlene. 'Suzie has earned her share of the glory. She caught one of the radiographers on the fiddle.'

'Yes,' said Suzie, sadly. 'Joan was the last person I'd have suspected.'

'What did she do exactly?' asked Gordy.

'She changed the stickers on the sets of X-rays.'

'But why?'

'To defraud insurance companies,' said Suzie. 'It all started when a friend of hers wanted to take out a life insurance policy, but needed a medical. Joan did the X-rays, but they showed a patch on

182

his lung and a couple of other problems.'

'Bad insurance risk,' observed Gordy. 'He'd never have been accepted.'

'That's why Joan helped him. The X-rays had to be sent to the consultant here whose services had been retained by the insurance company. He studied the X-rays and signed a paper to say that the patient had no chest problems.'

'But he had,' said Gordy.

'Yes,' explained Suzie, 'but the consultant never saw his X-rays. He saw a set belonging to somebody else. Joan changed the sticker on a set of X-rays of a perfectly healthy patient. Her friend got the policy he wanted, and gave Joan a hundred pounds for her help.'

'What a racket!' said Karlene.

'Joan got away with it three or four times. Dennis Reynolds was her latest. I remember thinking that he was a heavy smoker when I met him, but the X-rays that Joan sent off for him were completely clear. She used someone else's set, and put a sticker on with his name on them.'

'You caught her, Suzie.'

'Only by chance, Karlene. To be honest, I thought Hayley might be involved. But she wasn't. She was just distracted by all that business with Zack.'

'Hayley won't be distracted any more,' said

Karlene. 'She and Zack are back together again. He went to the doctor about his shoulder and got sent for an immediate test. It was a benign tumour. They're going to remove it.'

'Oh that's a relief!'

'Yes,' added Gordy, 'the malignant tumour was the so-called Doctor Carl Mullen.'

'Shhhh!' hissed Karlene. 'Bella's coming.'

They heard feet coming downstairs and Bella came in with Mark. She'd been very subdued since the night her boyfriend had been exposed as a fraud. The others had been very tactful with her and Bella was coming to terms with what had happened.

'While we're all here,' she announced, 'I just want to thank you for not rubbing it in. I was an idiot to trust Carl - or Liam, as he really was. He was so convincing and I have to admit, I was beginning to really care about him.'

'Nobody blames you,' said Mark. 'We're just grateful that he was found out. It's pathetic, really. He couldn't make it as a doctor himself so he pretended to be his brother.'

'Yes,' said Bella. 'He lived in a fantasy world.' She sighed heavily. 'So did I. It's taught me a lesson. In future, I'll send all my boyfriends to Suzie for an X-ray so I can see what they're *really* like.'

'As long as Joan doesn't do the X-rays!'

'Jasmine's the one I feel sorry for,' Bella went on. 'I should never have inflicted a fake doctor on her. I feel terrible about that.'

'All's well that ends well,' said Mark. 'Jasmine had a bouncing boy. Mother and baby are both doing well.'

'Yes,' said Karlene. 'And who was the father? Baz or Raphael?'

Bella giggled. 'Jasmine was teasing us all. She knew all the time it was Raphael. She really loves him.'

The sound of the doorbell rang through their laughter.

'That'll be Kirst!' said Gordy, rubbing his hands together. 'My X-ray vision tells me she's standing on the doorstep, longing for me. We're going off for a celebration. Just the two of us.'

He ran to the door and flung it open. Kirsty was there, but so was Dodo, the Dalmatian. The dog jumped up at Gordy and began to lick his hand affectionately. Everyone in the house fell about laughing.

'What was that about X-ray vision, Gordy?' said Mark.

CITY
HOSPITAL

NEW BLOOD

As soon as the ambulance stopped, its doors opened and the stretcher was lifted swiftly but gently to the ground. The small boy with the chubby face lay pale and motionless on his back. As one of the paramedics wheeled him into Casualty, another walked alongside, holding the plastic bottle that was attached to his arm by a tube.

Dr Damian Holt was waiting with a nurse in a bay that was curtained off by a plastic sheet. One look at the patient told him that the boy was in a critical condition.

Two lives hang in the balance at City Hospital - but Suzie's involvement in the first means her life is in danger too

CITY
HOSPITAL

FEVER

Bella was stunned. 'Mrs Elliott isn't *dead* is she?'

'Yes, I'm afraid so. We did all we could but...' Her voice trailed off – she looked shocked and confused herself.

'What was the cause of death?'

Sister Morgan's face changed. Bella had never seen her look like that before; a look of fear and bewilderment. It was as if she'd come up against something completely outside her experience. It scared her. She bit her lip and shook her head sadly.

'We don't know, Bella,' she admitted. 'We just don't know.'

Feelings run to fever-pitch at City Hospital – will someone crack under the strain?

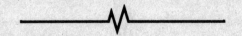

CITY
HOSPITAL

EMERGENCY

Out!' repeated Jez. 'Or she gets it!'

Two more security guards had arrived and were looking in through the window. They watched as their colleague slowly backed out of the office with the two male nurses. Jez Halliday held the advantage for the moment and there was little that they could do. Sister Poole and Bella Denton were hostages.

'Stay back!' he yelled. 'Or I blow her brains out.

A high-tension hostage situation puts the whole of City Hospital on edge – who will break the deadlock?

Order Form

To order direct from the publishers, just make a list of the titles you want and fill in the form below:

Name ....

Address ....

....

....

Send to: Dept 6, HarperCollins Publishers Ltd, Westerhill Road, Bishopbriggs, Glasgow G64 2QT.

Please enclose a cheque or postal order to the value of the cover price, plus:

UK & BFPO: Add £1.00 for the first book, and 25p per copy for each addition book ordered.

Overseas and Eire: Add £2.95 service charge. Books will be sent by surface mail but quotes for airmail despatch will be given on request.

A 24-hour telephone ordering service is available to Visa and Access card holders: 0141-772 2281